# GOD

# DARK WEB

# LUCAS MANGUM

deadite
press

DEADITE PRESS
P.O. BOX 10065
PORTLAND, OR 97296
www.DEADITEPRESS.com

AN ERASERHEAD PRESS COMPANY
www.ERASERHEADPRESS.com

ISBN: 978-1-62105-271-5

This book wouldn't have been possible without Jeff Burk and his enthusiasm for the concept, Shane McKenzie and his constant encouragement to push the envelope, or the YouTube channel, Dorset Ghost, whose dark web, cult and ghost stories made me want to tell a dark web horror story of my own.

*For Manderson*

# IT'S ABOUT TO GET DARK
## AN INTRODUCTION
## BY GABINO IGLESIAS

You're holding a Deadite Press book, so I know you have no problem with darkness. That's a good thing, my friend, because shit's about to get dark. Really dark. You see, Lucas Mangum is one of those authors whose love for horror is obvious. He loves the genre. He loves the books and the scene and the movies. He loves to scare people, to show them things they won't quickly forget, and his work reflects that. In fact, of everything he has written, this is the book that reflects it the most. Terror. Anxiety. Ugly things. Crippling fear. Screams. Torture. Explosions of bodily fluids. Confusion. Edge-of-your-seat tension. You name it, it's here. And that's just the first chapter. You see, Deadite Press is known for publishing hardcore horror fiction, and when they say hardcore, they're not messing around. Now that Mangum has joined the ranks of horror masters like Edward Lee, Wrath James White, Robert Devereaux, Brian Keene, J.F. Gonzalez, Bryan Smith, and Ryan Harding, we know he isn't messing around either. Oh, and you can go ahead and stop calling him a talented upcoming voice or a future horror household name; the dude has arrived.

Yeah, Deadite Press, for those brave enough to call ourselves horror fiction connoisseurs, means something, and getting a book published by Deadite Press places its author in a special group, a nasty, brilliant, unique group of writers who constantly push the envelope in all directions until the damn thing bursts and its pink, slimy guts go flying over our astonished heads. What you are currently holding is the thing Mangum created that got his name on that list of masters, and that makes it a once-in-a-career deal. I'm glad you're here to witness this. Also, you better hold on…and bring some tissues.

By now, if you belong to the truly enlightened crowd of those who read introductions, you may be asking "Okay, the book is good, but what is so special about it that you felt the need to finesse your way into writing this introduction?" Easy: this is what fast, dirty, smart horror should be. All of the writers I mentioned above belong to a different era. Mangum is the new wave. He has read those names in the first paragraph, and he has learned from them, he has paid attention and internalized the lessons hidden in those pages. The result is a book in which he drops readers into the middle of the action from the get-go and then steps on the gas until the last page. The only response to it is to keep turning the pages, to keep wondering, to keep cringing as the narrative moves forward at breakneck speed. It's truly a beautiful thing, and I'm sure it won't be the last time he does it. Why? Because Mangum, besides loving horror, is also a hustler. He sits down and puts words to paper. That's what a real writer does, and he is doing it better and better with each new book. I guess, in a way, I tricked him into letting me write an introduction so that when he is the newest hardcore horror sensation, I can hit him up for a blurb. Maybe I did it just so I can say I knew him back when he was relatively new in the game. Maybe I just felt like being part of something I knew would be special. Whatever. My hidden agenda shall remain hidden. The point is that you, dear reader, are in for something unusual, something exciting, and the fact that you're about to dig into the world of pain and brutality that Mangum cooked up for you makes me happy.

If you have read Mangum's work before, then get ready to read his best outing so far. If, on the other hand, you're encountering his depraved words here for the first time, then prepare yourself to read a novella that will place its author on your list of "buy everything they publish" writers. Yeah, this is that good. This is proof that the new generation of hardcore horror writers is ready to get filthy, to push on readers their own brand of debauchery and mayhem, to open a book with someone getting their face pissed on. Yeah, the kids are alright. Now enter the world of a writer you'll be talking about for a long time to come. Just be aware of what I already told you and revel in it: it's about to get fucking dark.

# 1

Leon awoke to pain. His head throbbed. His limbs ached. He tasted blood. The twin odors of ammonia and fertilizer stung his nostrils. Something wet and sticky dripped into his hair.

He opened his eyes. He was in an old, abandoned building of some kind. Crab grass and dandelions and a cherry blossom tree had grown up through the cracked concrete floor. Broken windows surrounded him on all sides, reminding him of mouths full of jagged, crooked teeth. Mildew and dirt darkened the cinder block walls. Strangest of all, the outdated, broken down electronic equipment filled the room, stacked on folding tables with rotting, bowed table tops, and scattered across the floor. Bulky computer monitors, keyboards and mice, receivers and speakers, circuit boards, and endless stretches of wires.

He tried to move, but couldn't. His hands were pinned behind him, tied to the back of a chair.

"Oh, God, what the fuck. *Help! Help! Someone please!*"

His cries rang hollow through the building, traveled out the windows to be choked by the outside woods. Another wet drop plopped into his hair. He glanced up. A bloated, pale figure hung above him. Two red nubs dangled from torn jeans. A concave face lolled from slumped shoulders, its eyes sunken, its bottom jaw removed, exposing a gray and pink tongue.

Leon screamed again. This time he rocked in the chair and spilled to the side, still restrained. He didn't stop screaming. Sometimes he formed words; other times he babbled and bellowed nonsense. He cried himself raw and took to quietly sobbing into the dirty floor. Blood from the legless corpse dripped onto the side of his pants, not ideal, but better than in his hair. He sniffed and drew a plume of moist dust into his nostrils, which itched and made him sneeze, sending more dust into his eyes.

"Fuck," he groaned.

Footsteps tromped the grounds outside. They sounded close. Leon detected two sets, one heavier than the other. At second thought, maybe more. A faint shuffling accompanied the steps. He cleared his throat and tried to work up the strength to scream for help again. The footsteps stopped outside the door.

"*Please!*"

Keys jingled. The knob turned. The door swung open toward Leon. He licked his lips. A fat drop of blood splashed onto his hip. He cringed.

Two figures dressed in gray, their faces covered by bulky Halloween masks entered the building. One wore a crimson devil mask. The other wore an enlarged skull. Each of them held leashes, dragging them behind their bodies. Belts hung from their hips containing all manner of knives and sharp objects. Skull's belt contained a gleaming revolver.

The leashes dragged two naked women by their necks. Pink scars in various stages of healing covered their bodies. Their unwashed, knotty hair bounced around their heads as they crawled inside the building.

Leon swallowed, blinked, and tried to assess his situation. All he came up with was, *I'm fucked.*

\*\*\*

Leon began to explore the deep web six months ago. Despite the lurid reputation garnered by the unindexed areas of the internet, the dark net's perceived anonymity made it a haven for activists who wanted to protect their identity. He and a group of friends had gotten involved in the local chapter of Peace Ponies a wide-reaching group that opposed war for profit, economic inequality, homo and transphobia, and sexual assault. They joined up after one of Leon's friends was raped on her college campus, and they used a password-protected, non-indexed forum to come up with ideas and plan protests. Since Leon went to Catholic school and his father was an ultra-conservative Gulf War veteran, Leon thought it best to keep his involvement in the radical group as secret as possible.

One night after a group of counter-protesters started a brawl at a rally outside Senator Charles Renner's office over the state's transgender bathroom bill, Leon and his friend, Shiloh, thought it might be a good idea to get a gun. Leon didn't care much for firearms, but the incident had spooked him enough to think maybe he might need one to defend himself if a protest turned violent again. Shiloh said sometimes simply showing a gun is enough to make someone reconsider starting any trouble. Both of them being seventeen, they had to get creative in their methods of obtaining a firearm. They turned to the deep web.

\*\*\*

The two masked figures descended the stairs into the building's main floor, leash-bound women in tow. Leon gritted his teeth and squirmed against his restraints. The masked figures stopped five paces away. The women stopped and leaned back on their haunches and brushed their hair from their faces. Purple and yellow bruises darkened their cheeks and eyes. Their split lips spread, exposing twin smiles full of broken teeth. Leon's stomach lurched. The woman on the right drooled blood.

The kick to the gut caught Leon off-guard. He should have expected something, but the whole situation had him rattled. Exhaustion put a damper on his reflexes. The kick stung, winded him. He wanted to free his arms and legs and wrap them around his abdomen, to curl up in a ball and catch his breath, but the restrains were too tight, probably professional. He winced and groaned against the pain.

The masked figures exchanged glances. The naked women with the broken teeth kept on smiling. Skull stepped forward and kicked Leon again and again and again, alighting his midsection with flares of agony. He tried to tighten his abs against the blows, but they came with too much force and in too great a quantity. He resolved to lie there prone until the kicks stopped. When they finally did, he wheezed in and out, tears blurring his eyes.

Skull returned to his place beside Devil. They again exchanged glances, but no words. The crazy naked bitches kept on grinning. Leon writhed on the floor, let loose a fresh succession of screams. Some of the electronic equipment started to turn itself on.

\*\*\*

After their attempts to acquire a firearm proved fruitless, Leon and Shiloh got bored and frustrated. Shiloh started clicking through links to pass the time. Shiloh said he took all the necessary precautions and Leon took the black tape over Shiloh's webcam as a testament to this. Leon had never explored the deep web beyond the Peace Ponies forum. Shiloh said he had messed around a little bit before, but not a lot.

Soon they were finding all kinds of sick shit. Execution videos, some of them clearly the work of ISIS, others of unknown origin. Genital mutilation. Child pornography.

("Dude, get off of that shit," Leon said when they came across naked photos of girls no more than ten-years-old in provocative poses. Sitting spread-eagle to show their hairless vulvas. Arms held above their heads, displaying undeveloped breasts. Wide-eyed stares revealing the full-breadth of their exploited naiveté. Shiloh giggled and said, "Okay, okay.")

After nearly an hour of exploring, they came across a site that was a series of photographs showing what appeared to be some kind of ghost town. Twentieth century homes stood in various stages of dilapidation, some of them partially burned. Overgrown lawns consumed mailboxes and ornaments. Vehicles covered in pollen and dirt sat on flat tires. A dead German shepherd lay in a gutter, its long-rotted insides spilled onto the pavement. The broadside of a church, with its stained glass windows smashed out and its detached door sprawled across its front steps, bore graffiti in black spray paint. A bulbous figure with stringy tendrils and mechanical parts protruding from its blobby center was drawn above the text, *WE WHO SHALL NOT BE NAMED.*

A chat box popped up on screen. *Hey.*

"Close it," Leon said.

Shiloh's cursor searched for something to click.

"I can't," he said.

*Do you like our town? I hope so. You'll be joining us one day.*

\*\*\*

As Leon lay on the cracked cement floor, agonized and humiliated, he thought this should be Shiloh enduring this. He's the one who kept exploring. He's the one who didn't take the proper precautions. He's the one who giggled at the fucking kiddie porn.

Another drop of blood splashed against his pants from

the hanging corpse. The electronics beeped and blinked to life. He recognized this place. This abandoned garage had shown up in the photo set from the abandoned town. The electronics had been inside, but not the hanging corpse and not these masked psychos and their slave women.

Devil pulled some kind of flogger from his belt and smacked it across the shoulder blades of his leashed companion. She got back on all fours and he drew the flogger across her ass cheeks. Her broken teeth sunk into her lips and she crawled forward. Leon tried to squirm away as she drew closer.

*Oh, God. What now? What the fuck now?*

She crawled over him, crouched above his head. Her pussy was chafed raw. The spray of urine splashed hot against his face. He closed his eyes and tried to turn away, but the piss soaked his hair, seeped through his lips and into his nostrils. He coughed and got another mouthful. When she finished, she crawled back to her master's side. Leon spat out as much pee as he could.

"Goddamn it. What the fuck? What do you assholes want?" he asked, knowing full-well what they wanted. They had been getting what they wanted since they brought him here and they would continue to get what they wanted, no matter how extreme, until he either escaped by some miracle, or he died.

\*\*\*

Days went by after Leon and Shiloh's failed attempts to attain a firearm, but the images from the deep web infected Leon's every thought. The memory of the execution videos made it difficult to work up an appetite. The images of the naked children made it difficult to get aroused and when his girlfriend, Dana, asked him what was wrong, he told her he wasn't feeling well, which wasn't entirely untrue. He felt dirty, as if entering these forbidden regions of the net had marked him somehow. Tainted him.

Later in the week, on his way to school, he noticed a rusty cream-colored car parked at the end of his street, where his neighborhood ended and let out onto the main drag. He thought nothing of it until he saw something spray painted on the hood, something that resembled the amorphous shape sprayed on the side of the abandoned church in the photos.

He didn't go home that night. He went to Maryann's Diner instead, told his dad and Dana that he needed to study. After hours of drinking coffee and trying to focus on his homework, he worked up the will to drive home, resolved that if he saw the car again, he would call the police immediately.

He remembered walking out to his car in the parking lot of Maryann's, then nothing. Next thing he knew, he woke up in this room, hands bound behind him, a legless corpse dripping blood into his hair.

***

More masked figures entered. A pig. A pumpkin. Someone in a Jason Voorhees mask. They gathered around as more of the machines blinked and beeped to life. Jason carried a nineteen-eighties boom box and set it down between Devil and Skull. He depressed the play button and stepped back.

First there was static. Then, distorted laughter, voices whispering, a synthesizer playing hypnotic, repetitive pattern. The two naked women bowed their heads and their knotty hair fell in front of their scarred breasts. The masked figures all held up their hands. Even Skull and Devil let the leashes drop. The sounds on the tape grew louder. Another drop of blood pattered on Leon's leg. Sour piss stung his eyes.

17

Pieces of electronic equipment shifted. Smaller, looser items fell to the floor. Computer monitors and hard drives pulsed as if they were breathing. The wires began to uncoil. Something orange glowed beneath the scattered debris.

Leon twisted his arms. He tried kicking his legs free. Fresh panic surged through his veins. He let loose a series of bellows that shredded the back of his throat. Someone had to hear him. Someone had to be close enough to hear him and have the sense to call for help.

The masked figures chanted with the whispers on the tape, the volume increasing, the rhythm becoming more frantic. Something crackled and whined. Leon couldn't tell if it came from the tape or from the pulsing, shifting equipment.

The wires lashed the floor, striking sparks against the concrete, cutting down overgrown weeds. The monitors displayed endless lines of green text and glyphs against black backgrounds. Items bounced and jerked, making sounds both electrical and organic, something squishing and tearing. Orange ooze seeped through the gaps between the equipment. The ooze glowed like neon lava and blue lightning sizzled through its extremities.

Leon continued to scream, bitter piss on his tongue, abdomen alight with pain, blood soaking the right side of his jeans. His arms and legs would not get free. He tried to convince himself he was having a nightmare, pleaded with himself to wake up, prayed to every god whose name he could remember.

But the god rising before him knew no mercy, nor compassion, nor loving kindness. The god before him was too old to feel those things. Though this god had clearly evolved, adapted in order to survive, its primal driving force remained intact: it demanded blood sacrifices and other acts carried out in its name. All who saw its face went mad, as mad as Leon, as arcing wires and gelatinous appendages dragged him laughing, weeping, and screaming into the old god's new mechanical jaws.

# 2

Niles Highsmith was signing a copy of his true crime bestseller, *The Tucker County Strangler*, when his father called to tell him Leon had gone missing. The signing was Niles's first public appearance since the dissolution of his marriage, since the death of his son. His father knew this, so Niles guessed the call had to be important.

"Excuse me," he said to a grimacing senior citizen with a blurry tattoo on his left arm that could have come from either prison or the military. "I have to take this. Sorry."

The old guy muttered something about kids and their cell phones, which was funny because Niles was in his thirties.

Niles ducked behind an endcap stocked with plush toys instead of books. It drove him nuts that all the big chain bookstores had taken to filling half of their shelves with things other than books. No wonder brick and mortar bookstores were in trouble. He continued to sign at this one, because he was friends with the manager and it was close to home and since it was the first place he had ever done a signing, it had sentimental value.

He pressed the answer button, held the phone to his ear, and covered his other ear with his finger to drown out the whiny pop music playing over the store's loud speakers.

"Dad, is everything okay?"

"It's Leon. Have you talked to him at all?"

Niles didn't worry at first. Leon and their father often butted heads, which led his little brother to take steps to avoid the old man. Usually, he stayed at a friend's house for a few days.

"No. How long's he been missing?"

"Over a week."

*Shit. That's not normal.* "Did anything happen?"

"You mean did I do something to *make* him run away?"

"Dad..."

"We had a fight, but nothing more explosive than usual."

"What was it about?"

"Christ, can we save that for when we talk to the cops?"

"You haven't called them yet?"

"No, wanted to see if he called you first. I know he looks up to you."

A hint of disgust entered his tone when he said the last sentence.

"Look, let me wrap up here and then I'll come over. Call the police."

Niles disconnected. He bumped into Dennis, the manager, on the way back to his table. Dennis frowned.

"Hey, everything okay?"

"Not really. It's family-related."

Dennis's features drooped. "Do you need to reschedule?"

"I think so. Brother's gone missing. It's not like him to be gone so long."

Dennis nodded, but his features remained sunken. Niles read disappointment in every line. He tried to push the guilt away and reminded himself that family, however fractured, came first.

# 3

"Did you call the police?" Niles asked when he walked into his father's house.

"Yeah, since he's been reported as a runaway before they had me do a report over the phone. You ever hear that kind of bullshit?"

"Did you tell them he had never been gone this long before?"

"Yeah, I did. Christ, how dumb you think your old man is?"

"Well, what'd they say?"

"They asked if he had any mental disorders. I asked them if liberalism counted." Niles's father laughed. Niles did not. "Anyway, they took the report and told me it will get assigned to a detective and they gave me a case number. Typical bureaucracy bullshit. I doubt they'll do anything to try to find him."

"Have you tried calling any of his friends?"

"No, maybe you could…"

"I can try," Niles said. "First tell me what you two fought about."

His father shrugged. "Wasn't much of a fight really. He was walking around the house all pissed off about something and he wouldn't tell me what. Finally told him he either tell me what's wrong or he needs to learn how to hide his emotions better."

"Nice," Niles said, thinking his father's ultimatum was anything but. Leon had actually called and told him about that fight, but that had been over *two* weeks ago.

"Shit, I was just trying to get a reaction."

"That was the last time you two fought?"

"Yeah, but he hadn't really talked to me since then, so I just assumed when he went missing he was still sore about what I said." His father leaned back and folded his hands. "So, you'll ask around? Doubt his friends would have shit to say to me."

*Probably true.* "All right, I'll ask around."

# 4

Niles first approached Leon's girlfriend, Dana. She agreed to meet him at the Maryann's Diner off of Route 13. He found her sprawled across a booth in the back, a ragged paperback with yellowed pages clutched in both hands. She lifted her gaze to meet him when he approached and offered him a smile. Something brightened in her eyes for a second and a half. Then the darkness returned, a cloudy quality brought on by an obvious lack of sleep. He hated seeing her like this. He'd always liked her.

Niles sat down. She set the book aside and leaned back. Niles shifted his attention to a mug of black coffee steaming in front of her. His mouth watered. He craved the beverage, despite not enjoying the taste all that much. It helped him stay sharp. At least he thought it still did. When the waitress came, he ordered a cup.

"How've you been?" he asked Dana.

Dana shrugged. "I'm as well as can be expected. It has been kind of weird since Leon disappeared. How about you?"

"I just found out he was missing this afternoon. Thought if anyone knew where he was, it'd be you."

"Sorry, Niles, I can't help you there." Her voice was scratchy. Low. It had the quality of a middle-aged woman who had spent her life smoking a pack of cigarettes every day. Niles guessed she had been crying. "I wish I could."

"When was the last time you talked to him?"

The coffee came. The raven-haired waitress asked if they were ready to order. They declined food, but had her leave a menu.

24

"We hung out a little over a week ago. It must have been right before he went missing. I could tell there was something wrong too." She shook her head. "I figured it had to do with the violence that broke out at the last Peace Ponies protest. It really shook him up."

"Yeah, heard about that."

"For being a writer, you sure like to use a lot of incomplete sentences."

"Guilty." She almost brightened. He could already tell he wouldn't get far with her. She didn't seem to know much more than he did, and he doubted she would hide information from him. He decided to ask anyway. "If he was staying with you, you'd fess up to me, right?"

She opened her mouth to answer, but he cut her off.

"Because I get it. Our dad can be difficult. Probably even more so if Leon was already under stress."

"He is not staying with me. I wouldn't lie to you about that. I can tell how worried you are."

"Good enough. Did he say anything else that was odd? Do anything else?"

She shrugged. "This is probably TMI, but he was pretty uninterested in sex before he disappeared."

"Guessing that's abnormal?"

She nodded. "Definitely."

Niles tried to wipe the image of his brother and this pretty, but underage, woman having sex. He sighed and sipped his coffee and missed his wife.

"I wish there was more I could tell you."

"Me too." His gaze wandered outside. Dark gray clouds were rolling in on the horizon. Rain sprinkled the diner's window. He set a twenty on the table. "Here, get some food. I'm gonna do some more digging."

She pushed the bill back to him. "What are you, my grandpa?"

He took back the bill. "Your loss. If you hear anything, let me know."

# 5

He tried Shiloh next. He showed up at the boy's house. Shiloh was notoriously bad at answering his phone. Shiloh's father answered the door and frowned.

"Help you with something?"

"I'm looking for Shiloh."

Shiloh's father took a step back and sized Niles up.

"You're not a cop, are you?"

"Definitely not."

Shiloh's father nodded for a long moment. Niles caught a whiff of marijuana from inside the house. *Lucky I'm not a cop.* Shiloh's father looked back and called Shiloh's name.

"Someone here to see you."

Niles wiped a spatter of raindrops from his forehead. "Mind if I come in?"

"Oh, yeah, no prob." Shiloh's father stepped aside.

Niles entered just as Shiloh stomped down the stairs. When he saw Niles, he frowned and it made him resemble a younger version of his father.

"You're Leon's brother, right?"

"Yeah, you mind if we talk?"

Shiloh's father jumped in. "No way, the writer? Man, *Tucker County Strangler*, some serious shit, man."

"Thanks."

"How hard is it to publish something like that?"

Niles gritted his teeth. He hated this line of questioning. Hated it even more when he had a specific agenda and someone's inquiries into the publishing world stood in his way. This was a minor annoyance when grocery shopping

27

or out on a date. He usually just smiled and gave his best canned answer, and went about his day.

"Hey, listen, don't want to be rude. My brother's missing and I'm wondering if your son has any information."

Shiloh's father deflated. Redness started to cloud his cheeks. Niles tensed. Shiloh stepped between them.

"Hey, man, come to my room. We'll talk up there."

Niles bypassed Shiloh's father and went upstairs to Shiloh's room.

"Sorry about that," Shiloh said.

Shiloh sat down on the bed, a mattress on the floor and unsupported by a frame. He tossed a pillow at Niles's feet.

"Sit there," he said. "Don't trust that desk chair."

Niles sat cross-legged and winced as his knees popped. That happened more often than not these days. Even though he ran every day and tried to keep in shape, parts of him just didn't want to work the way they used to work. Getting to his feet was going to be a bitch.

"I'm glad you came by. Feeling all wigged out the last week. Wish I knew where Leon got off to."

"You don't have any idea?"

"I have some ideas, but I dunno if you want to hear any of them."

"Try me."

"I dunno, man."

"Shiloh, I'm looking for my brother. He's family. Anything you can tell me will help. Does it have to do with the protest going off the rails at the senator's house?"

Shiloh averted his gaze. He fiddled with a loose string on his camo shorts.

"It's more than that, isn't it?"

Shiloh resumed eye contact. "I don't want to freak you out."

"Doubt you could make my day any worse."

Shiloh lowered his resumed playing with the string on his shorts. He wrapped it around his finger and unraveled it. Pinched it tight and tore it free.

"You ever hear of the deep web?"

"A little. I know it's got a bunch of sites not searchable by Google. I know some people use it to buy drugs. Also heard you can use it to hire a hitman." At this, Niles snorted. "I imagine the whole thing's overhyped."

"Yes and no. The hitman thing is mostly just rumors, but man, you can find some fucked up shit there."

"Like what?"

"All *kinds* of fucked up shit."

"So, what's that have to do with my brother?"

"Well, we used the dark net, another name for the deep web, to basically organize a lot of our protests and meetings."

"That's right. I remember him mentioning that."

Shiloh sighed and brushed his thick black hair out of his face. He shifted like he was sitting on something uncomfortable. Niles didn't think it was the thin mattress. He thought Shiloh was hesitant to reveal any further information to him or talk anymore about the deep web.

"All right, so, um, you know how the Peace Ponies protest went bad?" Niles nodded. "Well, we got kind of freaked out by it and thought it might be a good idea to get a gun."

"I can't imagine Leon with a gun."

"Yeah, me neither, but you know, desperate times and shit."

"How bad did the protest get?"

"I dunno, man. Lot of our friends got our asses kicked. One of them was hospitalized. Leon and me barely got away."

"Okay," Niles said. He wondered where this conversation was going, but didn't want to be rude. Shiloh seemed to trust him enough. He motioned for Shiloh to continue.

"Anyway, we started searching for someone local who could sell us a gun. Didn't really find anything, so we just started clicking around randomly. Shit, man. Ever want to lose faith in humanity? Go browsing the deep web. There's porn for every fucked up fetish out there. Nastiest sexual acts you can think of? There's a page with something ten times worse. You got people with backwards ass political views ranting and raving about assassinations you hope they don't have the resources or the balls to actually carry out. Snuff films that may or may not be real. Like I said, all *kinds* of shit."

Niles leaned forward. He made a mental note to do further research on the deep web. Figured it might make for an interesting book topic. In the next thought he cursed himself for thinking of writing when trying to determine his missing brother's whereabouts. Shiloh continued.

"We came to this one site that was just photos of a freaky abandoned town. And we got a fucking message. Someone said, 'I hope you like our town. You'll be visiting soon.'"

"Do you remember the name of the town?"

Shiloh chewed his lip, thought for a quick moment and shook his head. "Nah, man, sorry."

"So, you think this had something to do with Leon's disappearance?"

"Shit, I dunno. I mean, you hear stories about people exploring the deep web and disappearing. Always figured they were just rumors, urban legends or some shit, but still. I thought I took all the necessary precautions. I used TOR. I have black tape over my webcam. Fuck, man, I hope some *freak* didn't...I'm sorry, you don't need to hear that shit."

Niles shook his head. "So, what, that's it? Few days later he goes missing?"

Shiloh shrugged.

"Do you know what website had all those photos? Email

address of the person who messaged you? Browser history?"

"Nah, man. No real way to retrieve that shit. And the message was just a chat box that popped up on the website."

"You sure it wasn't just a standard greeting?"

"They fucking knew our names."

"What? How?"

"Fucking hackers, man."

"Shit. Can you tell the police what you told me? Here." He handed Shiloh a paper with the case number on it.

"I don't want them to confiscate my computer, man. Need that shit for school."

"We're talking about my brother's well-being."

"Shit, I know, but maybe this isn't even related."

"Maybe not, but we should probably explore every possible angle, right?"

"Yeah, I guess so."

"So, you'll call the police?"

Shiloh nodded, but Niles only half-believed him.

# 6

Niles hovered his thumb over Bella's name in his phone. He tried to rationalize not calling. He asked himself why Leon would have contacted his ex-wife. Sure, she had served as a source of stability during Leon's tumultuous early teens. She was the first to coax Leon into talking over his issues instead of bottling them. Tales of her activism had inspired him to follow a similar path. Yet, they had not spoken since the divorce. Niles saw no reason for Leon to contact her.

Another voice nagged him. It echoed his earlier words to Shiloh.

*Maybe not, but we should probably explore every possible angle, right?*

*Guess I should practice what I preach.*

He sighed and pressed the call button. He didn't expect her to answer. The feathery voice said his name. He tensed.

"What's going on?" she asked. Businesslike. Clinical.

"I'm just wondering if you've heard from Leon."

"Leon? Why? Is everything okay?" Less businesslike. Less clinical. Full of worry. More emotion than he had heard from her in almost two years.

"I don't know. Dad says he's missing. Friends don't know where he is. Thought maybe he would've called you."

"No, I haven't talked to him since..." She drifted off. "Well, you know."

"Figured I'd check." Silence passed between them. Only her faint breathing indicated she hadn't hung up. "So, how've you been?"

"Holding together, I guess. I see you have a new book out."

"Yeah, did my first signing in a long time today too. Trying to move forward, you know?"

"Yeah, hey, I don't know if I'm ready to do this yet."

"What?"

"You know what I mean. Be friends."

"I'm just making conversation."

"I know, but…you shut down after Simon. Closed yourself off when I needed you most. It still hurts. I don't know if that will ever stop."

Niles never cared much for the term, *broken heart.* Anything he experienced that should have caused the proverbial heartbreak made him sick to his stomach instead. He felt that sickness now. His guts threatened vomit that never came.

"I'm sorry," he said.

"I know you are, but that doesn't change anything."

"You're right."

"I should go."

"Okay. Let me know if you hear from Leon, and uh…" She hung up. "I love you."

# 7

Shiloh didn't look up when the first cluster of emails came through. He maintained focus on his video game. Some texts came through. A series of Facebook messages followed.

"What the fuck," he said.

He paused the game. He grabbed his phone. Seventeen new text messages. Almost thirty Facebook messages. Eleven emails. Most of them said the same thing.

*You fucking pervert.*

*Sicko.*

*Pedo-faggot.*

*You're going to hell.*

Most of the messages came from friends. Some of them even came from family. The least malicious message came from a cousin in Vermont.

*Dude, what the hell? Your account better have been hacked or I'm disowning your ass.*

He checked his sent messages and his heart sank. An email had gone out to all his contacts. The subject line read, *sorry but this is me.* Kiddie porn filled the body of the email. Naked children stretched and sprawled in provocative poses. He scrolled through the email, eyes unblinking, unable to look away. Little girls sucked dick at gunpoint. Grown women fellated chained up little boys. The photograph quality ranged from fuzzy cheap cell phone shots to borderline professional.

Shiloh remembered how he had laughed when he and Leon stumbled upon child pornography the other week. Now laughing was the farthest thing from his mind. His stomach turned in a mix of panic and revulsion as more condemning messages came through. He tried to power down his phone. His hands trembled. The phone slipped from his grasp and crashed to the floor. He backed away from it like someone had told him an Ebola patient had rubbed it on their hemorrhaging genitals.

His father yelled his name from downstairs. He froze. His father ascended the stairs. With each approaching footstep, Shiloh's dread deepened. He shrunk away from the door, flattened himself against the wall. The door swung open. His father stood in frame, cell phone held out for Shiloh to see one of the awful photos again, free hand clenched into a fist.

"Want to explain this one?"

"I don't know, Dad. I think I was hacked or something."

"You think? Is this what you're into? This why you never had a girlfriend? You're into little kids?"

Something snapped inside Shiloh.

"What the fuck, Dad? I just told you I was hacked. I didn't send that message."

His father stood unmoving, breathing heavy, his face so red Shiloh half-expected smoke to plume from his nostrils.

"Dad…"

"You were hacked?"

"That's the only way that could've happened, okay?"

"Well, how the hell did they get into everything? Phone, email, Facebook…you got a lot of explaining to do."

"I know. Just…I need to think."

"Yeah, me too. Maybe you should go for a walk."

"What are you kicking me out?"

"Don't ask me that right now."

"So, you don't believe me?"

"I said take a walk, Shiloh."

Shiloh sighed. His father moved out of the way. Shiloh stomped down the stairs and out into the night. The woods around the house used to grant him immense comfort, especially after the sun went down. They were so peaceful. Now, his charging pulse and nauseous dread made serenity impossible.

He bounded down the hill, away from his house. He nearly lost his footing, but forged ahead. He ran until he got too winded. The dark of the woods encircled him. His house and the other houses in the neighborhood had all but disappeared. Distance and insufficient light rendered them into blurry shadows.

He dropped to his knees. He put his hands to the sides of his head and inhaled deep and ragged. Worst case scenarios played through his mind. He might lose his job if his boss at the gas station got the message. Some of his family may not believe him when he tells them he was hacked. He would never live it down at school, regardless of the truth.

*My life is fucking over.*

Something moved somewhere in the surrounding woods. He raised his head and glanced around. The darkness obscured all but the closest trees from sight. He tried to get control of his breath. Tried to listen for any other suspicious noises.

Probably just an animal, he thought and regretted it immediately. He couldn't count how many horror movies he had seen where victims uttered such a line of dialogue, only to end up machete fodder in the next frame.

*Doesn't matter. I'm fucking dead anyway.*

Movement again. This time closer.

The wind whispered through the leaves. Nature's static rendered the other sounds of the night indistinguishable.

*But something is coming.* Plodding footsteps in the woods ahead confirmed it.

His cynical attitude melted away. Maybe he could somehow repair the damage caused by the email. Even if he couldn't set things right, at least he could have the option to take his own life. Chemical suicide was supposed to be painless. He just had to make sure he didn't endanger the people around him. If he had to die, let it be on his terms, not killed by some maniac in the woods.

"Who's there?" He hid his hand in his jacket pocket. "I have a gun. You better not come any closer."

The person or animal walking the woods did not heed his warning. The footsteps drew closer. He backed off.

"I mean it," he said, lips trembling, voice cracking.

The foliage parted. Two hooded figures stepped into the clearing. Branches clung to the arms of their sweatshirts. A lack of light made it appear as though the twigs and branches extended from the cuffs, in place of hands. Instead of shoes, tangled roots splayed out from under their pant legs. It *had* to be a trick of the light. Though their faces were obscured, they had to be staring at him.

"Oh, fuck this noise."

He turned. To hell with Dad. He couldn't just throw Shiloh on the street.

Shiloh's footsteps stuttered. Two more hooded figures stood before him. Twisted branch arms stretched from each hoodie's sleeves. Gnarled roots gripped the forest floor. One hoodie raised their head.

Despite the branches stuffed into the hoodie cuffs and the nest of roots for feet, he still expected to see a human face. Instead, the raised hood revealed a black void filled with bright green characters. Numbers and strange glyphs moved vertically across the inside of the hood. He tried to look deeper, but the characters hypnotized him. Something primal inside him understood their pattern, the code, but he could only express its meaning by screaming.

# 8

After his confrontation with Shiloh, Graham had busted out a bottle of Maker's and drank half of it. Now a hangover compressed his mind. With it came the guilt. *Damn, I'm a shitty father sometimes.*

Sure, he had been upset, but maybe he should have given Shiloh the benefit of the doubt. He had seen on the news that hackers were capable of all kinds of crazy shit. Still, those photos had wounded him to his core. The fact they had come from his son's email address shook him up bad.

*Either way, it's a shitty situation.* Not everyone was going to believe Shiloh. Some of the more conservative members of their family wouldn't understand. Shiloh's boss almost definitely wouldn't. *Surprised no one called the police yet.* Maybe someone had. Maybe Shiloh was already on the books as a suspected child pornographer.

Graham stumbled out of bed and crossed the hall to Shiloh's room. He knocked on the door. When no one answered, he knocked again and pushed the door open. Shiloh was not inside. He hadn't come home from the walk Graham sent him on.

"Ah, shit."

He staggered downstairs and pushed his way out the door. The sunlight temporarily blinded him and he winced. His head throbbed, a nice reminder that he was too old to drink half a bottle of bourbon to himself. He couldn't hold his liquor like he used to. When his vision returned, he tottered down the hill to his Ford F150.

Graham started the truck and drove the winding road that

wove through the wooded neighborhood. His son liked to walk the trails. Though Graham couldn't totally gauge how much time had passed since he told Shiloh to take a walk, he figured the woods would be a good place to start searching.

Several times during the excursion, he tried Shiloh's cell phone. The calls went straight to voicemail. Anxiety set his nerves on edge. No longer just a fuck-up of father, he was a very worried fuck-up of a father.

He drove on and peered between the trees along each side street. He hoped to see something, anything, that would lead him to his boy. It had just been him and Shiloh in the seven years since Carol walked out on them. The boy was all he had. How could he not give Shiloh the benefit of the doubt? He cursed himself as he pulled down a cul-de-sac.

Graham brought the pickup truck to a screeching halt. His son hung from a tree toward the back of the cul-de-sac, in front of an unoccupied house. A leather belt was cinched around his neck. Lengths of intestine dangled from an angry red gash in his lower abdomen. Something brown and wet soaked his shoes and lower pant legs. The words *I am a pedo-faggot* were written on the empty home's white wall in what Graham could only assume was Shiloh's blood.

# 8

Dana called Niles crying. *She's going to tell me something happened to Leon. Why else would she be calling?*

"Dana, what's wrong? What is it?"

She told him about Shiloh. About the pornographic email all of Shiloh's friends received the night before. How Shiloh had been found dead in the woods, disemboweled and hanging from a tree.

"They think it was suicide," she said.

"How'd he manage to cut himself open before the hanging?"

"I don't know. They found a knife in the grass beneath his body. It had his prints all over it."

"Jesus."

"Yeah, right." She sniffed. "Did you get to talk to him before?"

"Right after I spoke with you."

"Did he seem off?"

"Not abnormally so. Considering my…considering Leon's his friend, I'd say he seemed as *off* as could be expected."

"This fucking sucks." Her voice cracked when she said it.

"Tell me about it." He paused to grind his teeth and think for a moment. "Hey, listen, do you know anything about the deep web?"

"I know a little. I have even gone on it a few times, but it's kind of creepy. Leon and Shiloh used to go on it to chat with the other Peace Ponies."

"Know how to get on it?"

"I know you have to download TOR. Make sure your mic is off and your webcam is blocked. You do not want any of the creepers to be able to identify you in any way."

"Why not?"

"Trust me. I think that might have happened to Shiloh. He could have gotten careless, and got his computer and phone hacked."

Niles remembered what Shiloh said about the message sent from the website showing the abandoned town.

"Do you think that's what happened to Leon?"

"I wish I knew. Shiloh dying like that while all this is going on just makes everything a lot worse."

"I know. I'm sorry."

"You did nothing to be sorry over."

"Well, Leon's listed as a missing person. Hopefully the police will be able to find him. If not, in the meantime, I think I'll check out the deep web. Maybe I can retrace some of his and Shiloh's footsteps."

"Just be careful, Niles. The dark net is full of creeps."

\*\*\*

Niles downloaded TOR, covered his webcam with black tape, and switched off his microphone. The first page was just a series of links. He clicked on the third one down. The link opened to a GIF. A yellow, bug-eyed cartoon pulled down its pants to moon him, and then looked over its shoulder to offer a white-gloved middle finger, while it grinned with ginormous square teeth. All the while its yellow butt wiggled.

Niles hit the back button. Wishing he knew where to start, he clicked another random link. It led to a page filled with indecipherable code. He scrolled until he found *ur a 8===D* written in neon green font halfway down the page.

*You're a dick. I kind of feel like one.*

He clicked out of the page and shook his head. This could take forever.

He tried searching for Peace Ponies. Nothing came up. He couldn't remember the name of the forum they used. He thought searching for someone to buy a gun from might work, but remembered Shiloh said they had been unable to find anyone, so that was probably a dead end. Like this.

*No, this isn't a dead end. This has too many possible ends and I don't even know where the hell to start.*

He resolved to browse aimlessly. At least he could do some research. At least he wouldn't feel ideal. Maybe he would come across something for his next book. Hoping to find a lead on Leon was wishful thinking at best. The deep web was big, vaster than the indexed portions of the internet. *And unless you know exactly what you're looking for, you're pretty much out of luck.* But still, maybe he would stumble upon something.

He had an inkling of hope. Foolish though hope may be, it had done him well in the past. After Bella left, when he was at his lowest, on a night he was halfway through writing a suicide note, hope came to him in the form of an email. The message came from a woman named Barbara whose daughter Julie had been a victim of the Tucker County Strangler. She thanked him for writing the book. She said he handled the subject with incredible care and never wandered into exploitative territory. The book had helped her find some closure from her daughter's death.

Looking back now, the email from the victim's mother seemed such a little thing, but then it brought him back from the brink. He tore up his suicide note. He dumped out all the liquor bottles in his house. He began the research that would grow into his second novel, *The Butcher of Hill Country*.

The fact that his work had helped a bereaved parent of

one of the Strangler's victims gave him hope. Her email had come to him at random. Maybe some tip on his brother's whereabouts would come at random.

He clicked another link. The page told an urban legend about a cursed screenplay, where everyone who attempted to direct it either died or went insane. Crime scene photos from each production's set were scattered through the text-heavy site. He had heard of some of the filmmakers and cast members. The last failed production had been spearheaded by William Ward, whose film, *Atrophy*, was a favorite of his. The page made a compelling argument, especially given that it named familiar figures and events, but by the end Niles dismissed it. Typos littered the page. The author went on tangents about Hollywood cults and the Illuminati and President Obama being a lizard. It's hard to earn credibility when you think the president is a lizard.

Another page led to a pornographic video where a counter at the bottom of the screen ticked off every time the woman screamed, "Oh, yeah." The counter reached one-hundred-sixty-seven by the time Niles clicked off of the page. It showed no sign of slowing down.

The next link he clicked brought him to a grainy black and white video showing the exterior of a house. Shot in first-person-POV, the camera moved forward. It bounced up and down with the cinematographer's footsteps. The camera reached the top of the front porch, and turned to scan the surrounding yards and the street. With the coast clear, the cameraman pushed open the front door and walked inside. A long hallway stretched ahead. Old sconces lined the walls.

Something hissed a phrase in a language Niles didn't understand. A woman wearing a white dress, eyes and mouth leaking black fluid stood at the opposite end of the hallway. She crammed her fingers into her midsection, clawing through the dress's fabric, clawing through skin and spilling black blood. She dug inside and pulled out a length of intestine with her right hand. With her left hand, she lifted her dress, exposing a hairy cunt between two pale thighs. She stuck the end of the intestine inside the thatch of pubic hair, into her vagina. Her black eyes rolled back, turned white. Her black tongue lolled.

Niles clicked the back button. He closed his browser. *That's enough for tonight.*

His phone rang. He reached for it. Leon's number showed on the lit up screen.

"Hello?"

Static responded.

"Leon, is that you?"

The static's hiss didn't change its tone.

"*Leon.*"

The line went dead. He called the number back. It went straight to voicemail.

"It's Leon. Leave a message."

"Leon, you just tried to call. Are you okay? Call me, man. We're all worried."

He hung up and leaned back in his chair. He closed his eyes and tried to catch his breath. The disemboweled woman masturbating with her own intestine tainted his mind's eye.

# 10

Niles couldn't sleep. He groaned and tossed off the blanket. He rolled out of bed and stomped to his study, muttering curses. Plopping in his office chair, he stared at his computer before switching it on. He checked Facebook, Twitter, and his email. He browsed Tumblr for porn and thought about jerking off, but didn't feel very horny. The clock showed it was a little after two in the morning. The computer monitor bathed the dark room in pale blue. He opened a Word document and rested his fingers on the keyboard. He crossed his left leg over his right and his left foot started shaking.

*Jittery. Why am I so goddamned jittery?*

Niles opened TOR. The same page of untitled links greeted him. He began to click. More of the same content from before filled his screen. Political rants. Creepy ghost videos (though none half as visceral as the disemboweled woman). Various types of pornography. Sophomoric GIFs.

He scrolled through absently. He shifted his position several times. Nothing felt comfortable for long. Finally he crossed his legs so tight they wrapped around each other. His shoulders pressed up against his neck. Labored, heavy breaths tore through his chest and windpipe. It felt like the onset of a panic attack.

He untwisted his legs, leaned back and tapped his fist against this desk.

A webpage opened. He hadn't clicked anything.

A paused video, titled "Smile," filled his monitor. He reached for his mouse, thought about clicking 'play,' and decided to close out instead. Only the website would not close. He clicked the 'x' again and again, but nothing happened. The video began to play.

A woman sat on her knees. Her dark hair hung in ringlets over her nude, pale shoulders. The camera gave a perfectly framed angle of her firm tits. Her eyes were wide and staring, seductive and expectant. She was licking her lips.

An erect penis entered the frame. A hand reached in and closed over its shaft. Started jacking. The woman kept licking her lips like the dick contained water and she'd been trudging through the desert for hours without it.

"Please," she moaned and whimpered. "Please."

Niles's own cock stirred at the image. He hated his mounting arousal. The video was misogynistic. He knew that even if his genitalia couldn't care less. As he hardened, his hand slipped to his lap. He unzipped and started stroking. The warmth of his hand helped him relax, refocused all that jittery energy on getting himself off to the sexual image. He tried to match the cameraman's rhythm.

The onscreen cock shot cum all over the woman's eyelids, cheeks, and lips. Niles's own orgasm lingered behind. His muscles contracted. The woman started to lick the semen. A fist swung into frame and smashed against the side of her cheek. Niles jolted. He came, but wished he could take it back.

The woman's head hung off to the side, hair covering her face. The cameraman remained over her, his penis softening. Niles's heartbeat accelerated. He felt it in his throat, his chest, his guts, his groin.

The woman spat blood and teeth into her lap. She lifted her head. She tossed her hair aside, revealing her face. Blood painted her chin red, mixing with blobs of cum. Her lips spread, revealing a smile full of broken teeth.

Niles unplugged his computer.

# 11

Niles called the police and gave the call taker the case number given to his father. He told them about Leon's exploration of the deep web. He told them about Shiloh's hesitance to talk to police before the suicide.

He didn't tell them about his own excursions into the deep web, or about the "Smile" message. Something held him back.

"Okay, we'll add that information to the case and make sure the detective sees it." The call taker's voice was masculine, but soft and tired. He said his name was Freddy, badge number

6520.

"Shouldn't someone pick up my brother's computer?"

"If the detective needs it, they'll get in contact with you or your father," Freddy said and confirmed Niles's phone number.

"Yeah, thanks."

Niles disconnected. He held the phone in his lap. He cast a wary glance at his computer before leaving the study and returning to bed. As he drifted toward the thresh sleep, he told himself he wouldn't go back on the deep web. The craggy-toothed grin of the woman from the last video haunted him. Dared him to look again.

# 12

Niles called Dana the next morning.

"Well, Niles, what do I owe the pleasure?"

"Just checking in. Everything okay?"

"I think you know the answer."

"Yeah." He scratched the back of his head, suddenly feeling stupid.

"How about you? Are you okay?"

"Didn't sleep much. Did some digging on the deep web. You weren't kidding. Found all kinds of weird shit. No sign of Leon though."

"I would not expect you to find any sign of him. Ninety-six percent of the internet is buried there, below the search engines. Hey, you are protecting yourself, right?"

"Think so. Using TOR. Got my camera covered."

"I thought of something after we talked. You will want to make sure you aren't running any scripts too. Those can give away your location and other information."

"Shit, really?"

He must have sounded extra spooked because Dana cleared her throat and her tone got serious.

"Niles, what did you find?"

He thought of both videos. The masturbating disemboweled woman. And *Smile*. "You probably don't want to know."

"You are probably right. Has anything weird happened?"

"Weird?"

"You know, weird. Have you gotten any suspicious emails or phone calls? Have you seen any strange cars in the neighborhood?"

"Jesus, no, but I just woke up." He went to his window and scoped out the street. "No, I don't think so. Jesus, Dana, is the risk really that great?"

"So I have heard. Of course you never know what to believe. Everything is still so shrouded in mystery. With Leon going missing and Shiloh's suicide, I guess I am a little more on edge than usual."

"I know what you mean." The dark-haired woman lifted her head. Smiled with broken teeth. He remembered how he had masturbated to her debasement before the cameraman struck her across the face. He felt dirty. "Anyway, I think I'm done with it. Not like I'll find anything."

"That might be a good idea, even if you are protected."

"Yeah, I won't be going on there anymore."

\*\*\*

Niles kept his word until that night. He hovered the cursor over a video titled, "Food Prep." He chewed his lip and tapped his foot. He contemplated not clicking through. There was no telling what waited for him beyond the link. He didn't think the video could be any worse than "Smile," but had no way of knowing for sure. Until last week, he had heard rumors about the deep web and how it was a dark place, populated by weirdos, bizarre imagery, and offering access to drugs and even hitmen. Everything he had heard did nothing to prepare him for the depravity lurking in the web's more shadowy corners. Even as a true crime writer, the things he had seen so far challenged his hardened sensibilities.

But still, he was no closer to finding Leon. That fact alone made him click the link, not that he expected to find anything. So far, his search had been one long guessing game, where the contestant got trolled hard for providing the wrong answer.

The video loaded and opened on a grainy shot of a cutting board. Deep grooves and dark stains indicated the board had gotten a lot of use. Somewhere in the background, a baby was crying.

A thick-fingered hand with dark hair covering the knuckles and wrist set down a red pepper. A kitchen knife entered the frame. The knife cut the pepper in half. The hand removed the seeds and stem. The knife cut the pepper into thin strips and then into tiny cubes, which the hand swept to the edge of the cutting board and dumped into a large, steel pot.

Niles watched as the videographer cut up three carrots, a tomato, an onion, a large potato, and a clove of garlic. Since both hands were used, Niles guessed the camera was mounted on the videographer's shoulder. The video bored him, but he was over-caffeinated and sleep-deprived, so he continued to view what seemed to be no more than an unseen cameraman preparing some kind of stew. All the while the baby cried in the background.

The hands carried the pot to the sink, filled it with water, and carried it to the stove. The videographer upended a cylindrical container of salt into the water, and turned on the stove. The camera turned, showing a kitchen full of antique cabinets, dusty counters, and sides of jerky hanging from hooks. A yellowed, once white, basinet sat blocking the doorway at the opposite end of the kitchen. The camera peered over the edge, revealing a naked baby boy, red-in-the-face crying and flailing its limbs. Shit and piss stained the mattress below.

The cameraman lifted the baby out of the crib and carried him back to the cutting board.

Niles shook his head. *No. No way.*

He moved the mouse cursor over the icon to close the window. The baby writhed on the cutting board as a rusty meat cleaver entered the frame.

"Oh, God," Niles said through gritted teeth.

He clicked the red x, but the window wouldn't close. He sucked in a sharp breath. His whole body tensed, then went numb as the cameraman raised the blade and buried it into the baby's shoulder. The baby shrieked as blood pooled around the wound and ran in three rivulets across his chest. The meat cleaver retracted with a sickening squelch, exposing stringy gristle and gleaming white bone. Another strike broke bone and split more skin. The arm hung on by a flap of skin, dangling over the edge of the board. The cameraman set down the cleaver and yanked off the arm and dropped it in the pot, turning the water red.

The infant's flailing decreased in speed. The red in his face drained, becoming a ghastly pale. His eyes stayed wide with panic, his cries choked with blood. He was aware only of the pain and the cruelty to which it was dealt to him. As his life slipped away, he may have been too young to understand his own mortality, but on some primal level, he had to know he was in some kind of danger. Had to fear what his agony meant.

The cameraman brought the blade down again, this time digging a bloody ditch in the opposite shoulder. This time, the blow came with more velocity and Niles could hear the blade scrape against bone.

Niles tried the red x several more times, but the window still wouldn't close. A second blow cut all the way through the other arm, thudded against the cutting board. Blood pooled around the severed limb. Niles tried pressing control, alt, and delete to no avail.

The baby's writhing became an intermittent twitch. The life in his eyes dimmed, except for a residual impression of horror. Niles tried the power button, but the computer stayed on.

"Mother fucker...son of a bitch...fuck..."

The cameraman dropped the baby's other arm into the stew with a plop. The water was boiling now, bubbling crimson, both severed arms bobbing up and down, a nightmare witch's brew.

Niles shoved himself out of his office chair and scrambled to the other side of the room to unplug his computer. He yanked the cord from the wall and the monitor went dark. He slumped against the wall and exhaled a ragged sigh. He was shaking, soaked in sweat, heart hammering like a rapid-fire, brass-knuckled fist. His guts heaved. His whole body jerked. Bile burned the back of his throat, but no vomit came.

The memory of the night Simon died slammed into his brain like a speeding, out of control car striking a guardrail on the highway. Niles had been in his study, working on a follow-up to *The Tucker County Strangler*. A couple of sentences into the thirty-first page, he heard Bella scream from upstairs. He jolted out of his chair and ran toward the sound, toward screams that did not stop.

Little Simon lay in his crib, not breathing. A pool of blood soaked the mattress. His child's baby blue eyes stared without seeing.

He remembered the 9-1-1 call. Bella, hysterical, tried to tell the operator what had happened. Niles took over, calm at first, but the emotion charging below the surface erupted after the dispatcher asked if the baby was breathing. He sobbed into the phone, slumped against the wall of the nursery, much like he now slumped against the wall of his study. Grief crushed him like deep sea water pressure, burying him into a dark, cold place he still, three years later, had not escaped.

Niles started stress breathing like his therapist had taught him. Deep breath in, hold for five seconds, and let out slowly. He couldn't stop shaking. Tears blurred his eyes.

He had seen hell, or the closest thing to real-life version, so much worse than anything imagined by would-be prophets and preachers. The more he thought of this, unable to wipe the twin superimposed images of the crying, mutilated baby and the stiff, unbreathing Simon, he thought the word *hell* didn't do that level of suffering justice. Hell was a story that conjured up enough fear to inspire devoted followers of religions that promised an alternative, although nowadays, in this enlightened age, it had been reduced to a trope in cheap horror movies or the stage show of heavy metal bands. Something goofy, to be enjoyed with a sense of irony.

No, from everything he had seen, the deep web was the new hell, the new underworld. It was a place where all of humanity's demons could play without fear of repercussions.

He wanted to believe what he'd seen wasn't real. Maybe the filmmaker had access to good special effects. He doubted it. The filmmaker used a late 1990s, early 2000s digital camera, which suggested he couldn't afford the materials to make a mutilation look so real. There was no fancy camerawork, no cutaways. Even given all that, Niles felt as if such a scene appeared on the deep web, it had to be real. Otherwise, why hide it? Why not post it on YouTube to showcase your special effects talents?

Niles' phone beeped, indicating an email. Almost a full minute passed before he could move. Paralyzing dread held him in place. To move, to rise to his feet, meant to reinsert himself into a world far uglier than he ever imagined. The acts committed in the "Food Prep" video and "Smile" and the executions far exceeded anything figures like the Tucker County Strangler had done. Maybe it was the act of seeing the violence take place that made him feel this way, but he didn't think so. What disturbed him most about the graphic images on the deep web was that collectively, along with the pornography and the danger of exploring these dark regions without taking necessary precautions, all seemed to have a philosophy. This shared belief encouraged the denizens of the dark net to push boundaries, to stay hidden from the rest of the world, to be their most twisted, depraved selves and indulge their darkest fantasies.

Niles rose to his feet and swiped his phone off his desk. The sender of the email was a string of numbers and characters. There was no subject; there wasn't even a domain name. He opened the message.

*u enjoy learn 2 make baby blood stew lulz*

Niles tensed. The phone's monitor darkened. He pressed the button to illuminate it again. He needed to see the message a second time to confirm its existence. The message showed on the display, unchanged.

*Fuck.* He thought he had protected himself sufficiently, but somehow, one of these freaks had gotten his email address. He dialed 9-1-1. He told the dispatcher what he saw. He told them about the message. They told him they would forward the information along, but without an actual web address or email address, their resources would be limited.

"In other words, someone can just…chop up a baby and post it on the internet and get away with it?"

"Sir, I understand you're upset. We might be able to see if there are any cases of missing infants, and maybe we can pinpoint something from there, do you remember anything distinct about the baby?"

"Just…just the pain that he was in," Niles said.

The dispatcher asked if he would be willing to meet with an officer. Niles said that would be fine. He disconnected and collapsed into his office chair. He rubbed his eyes and fixed his gaze on his computer, its screen dark. He had made his living working on that machine, but now he saw it in an ominous light. No longer a tool on which to build his livelihood, it loomed before him as a gateway into the forbidden.

# 13

Niles sat at a bar for the first time in a year. The Wet Wench Inn was dimly lit and smelled like yeast. Aside from two women holding hands in a booth and a burly man down the bar wearing a red cap, Niles was alone. A tall woman wearing black approached him from the opposite side of the bar. She asked what he wanted.

His hands shook as he ordered the first Lone Star and shot of Jack. He kept his head down. Each drink felt heavy, like a thirty-pound kettle bell. But the smell. God, the smell brought him back.

He didn't remember those last days, when he had been a long-term resident of Rock Bottom. He remembered nights he drank himself numb. When the void left by Bella's absence and the dagger of grief brought by Simon's death felt far away. There were other nights, too, when the drinking helped him remember. When remembrance cranked the agony up so high, he managed to transcend it, to achieve a euphoric state. For just. One. Night.

The subsequent hangover always brought more tears.

That didn't matter right now. What mattered was the nightmare. The very real nightmare he now inhabited. He had to drown it out.

He slammed the shot of whiskey and chased it with a pull from the longneck. His stomach burned and he expected to throw up. Instead, he belched. Warmth spread through his core. He nursed the rest of the beer so as not to get cut off early.

He ordered another round. And another. By the fourth beer-shot combo, his head was swimming. The bartender told him what his tab had reached and he waved her off. He felt sloppy, but electrified, every nerve abuzz.

The nightmare still remained. The image of the suffering baby played on a loop. It far eclipsed 'Smile' in terms of vile depravity. It made the disemboweled woman, which was possibly fake to begin with, seem tame. Baby's Blood Stew. The words floated through his thoughts like spoken poison.

By last call, Niles could barely stand. The bartender sized him up and asked if he needed her to call a cab.

"No, I'm good," he said and gave her a thumbs-up. "I got this."

He fumbled his phone out of his pocket and stumbled out the door. He dialed Bella. She answered on the second ring.

"Niles?" She sounded like his call had awoken her. "What's going on?"

Now that he had her on the phone, he didn't know what to say. He had a hard enough time figuring out why he had called her at all. Stupid thing to do. He considered hanging up. He leaned against the front wall of the Wet Wench.

"Niles, are you there?"

"Yeah, I'm here. Sorry."

"You're drunk."

"Smart girl. Knew I had a reason to love you."

"You must be *really* drunk. Have you heard from Leon?"

"Leon? Leon." He was slurring, fading in and out of consciousness. "I haven't heard from Leon. Still missing."

She sighed on the other end. "Are you...what are you doing?"

"Talking to you. Need to talk to someone. I saw something. Fucked me up."

"What'd you see?"

"I don't know. Fucked up shit. Fucked up. Fuck."

"Niles, I don't have time for this. I have work in the morning. I need sleep. You do, too, so go to bed."

She disconnected. He called her back and she didn't answer. At the beep he left a message.

"Bella. Bellaaaahhh." He laughed without humor. "Bella, I'm sorry. So fucking sorry about everything. About Simon. About us. Sorry I'm so trashed right now. Thinking. I don't know what I'm thinking. Just pick up, okay? Want to talk to you."

He disconnected and waited. When he thought enough time passed for her to listen to his message, he called back. Straight to voicemail. He hung up. Through blurred vision, he skimmed through his recent calls. He tapped Dana's number and dialed it.

She answered, sounding as sleepy as his ex-wife.

"Hello?"

"Dana, it's Niles."

"Niles, you sound toasted. You okay?"

He laughed with a little more humor than before. "Caught you."

"What?"

"Using a sentence fragment."

"At two in the morning, I think you can give me a break. What are doing?"

"Your suspicion is not unfounded. I am drunk."

"I can tell."

"Yeah…"

"Where are you? Do you need a ride?"

"Maybe? You ever hear of the Wet Wench?"

"I have. Is that where you are?"

"Yeah."

"Give me some time to get dressed. I will pick you up. Do not drive."

"Yes, ma'am." He saluted to no one that could see.

By the time she arrived, he had slid to his knees and passed out against the building. A honk of the horn awoke him and he watched her silver Acura pull up to the curb. His vision spun. It took him a few seconds to register who the person in the car was and why they were getting out to approach him. Dana crouched in front of him.

"Jesus, Niles. You really tied one on, as the cool kids say."

He nodded. Bile burned the back of his throat. His stomach felt like it contained a hurricane. He lurched to his feet, using the wall and Dana's shoulder for support. She led him to the passenger side and opened the door to let him fall into the seat. When he got buckled in, she drove away from the Wench.

"You need to tell me where you live."

He slurred his address.

"No, sir, you need to stay awake and point me in the right direction. The GPS eats up all the data on my phone."

"Ten-four, good buddy."

She chuckled and shook her head. "Why did you get so trashed?"

"It's long story."

"I have time if you want to talk about it. It has been a hard week. You could probably use a shoulder. I guess I could too."

"Something I saw on the deep web. Got a weird message afterward, asking if I liked what I'd seen."

"Did you stop running scripts and plug-ins like I told you?"

"Uh huh."

"What did you see?"

"Someone chopped up a little baby and mixed him into a stew."

"Oh my God. Do you think it was real?"

He put down her window and vomited. The puke sprayed along the side of the car. Some splattered the asphalt. The wind carried the rest of it.

"Should I take that as a yes?"

He wiped his mouth and slumped into the seat. The car fell silent. The silence had weight.

"Turn here," he said, thankful for the sound.

For the rest of the ride, they exchanged no more words, except when he directed her to his home. She parked in the driveway.

"I heard about what happened," she said. He didn't reply. "Two years ago. Your son."

She was using incomplete sentences, but he no longer felt like joking. A wave of sobriety rose within him. But it was desperate sobriety. Cold. Ugly. Full of fear.

"It's fine," he said. "There's nothing I could have done. It was two years ago."

He sounded like a recording, repeating the same clinical phrases he had taught himself in order to reach a level of understanding and acceptance. The words tasted worse than the vomit.

"It's not fine," she said. Something warm encircled his fingers. She was holding his hand. "It's not fine, and it's okay for you to not be fine."

A sob tore loose from somewhere deep inside of him and it brought a barrage of others. Hot tears stung his cheeks. He closed his eyes and leaned into Dana. She wrapped him in her arms. She let him cry.

All dried out and raw, with the agony cranked up to eleven, he had reached that transcendent state. A catharsis greater than any artificial high overtook him. He pulled out of Dana's embrace, locked his gaze onto hers, and moved in for a kiss. His lips mashed against her fingers.

"None of that, sir. You are almost old enough to be my dad."

"Come on, it's okay."

He grasped her hand and kissed her fingertips. She pulled away.

"Niles, no. You are in major creep territory right now."

"Hey, look, I'm just…" *Just what.* Just very fucking drunk. Beyond drunk. Hammered. Shitfaced. "Oh, fuck. I, uh, should probably go."

"If you don't want pepper spray in your eyes, I think you're right."

Her features were hard, unmoving. He turned away and pushed his way out the passenger door and staggered up his front stoop. He blacked out before he reached his bedroom.

# 14

Niles awoke to pain. His temples throbbed. Acid ate away at the lining of his stomach. Every limb felt weighted down. Pieces from the night before came to him. Calling Bella in a drunken stupor. Trying to kiss Dana. He wanted to go back to the bar and keep drinking. Keep drinking until he existed in a permanent blackout state. Until he died passed out in a puddle of his own puke and never woke up.

*I'm done. Done with the deep web. Done looking for Leon.*

He would decide if he was done drinking later, after he decided if he still wanted to live.

He left apologetic messages on Bella's and Dana's answering machines. He ended both messages the same.

"I get it if you never want to talk to me again."

He hung up and his phone beeped. The email icon blinked at the top of the screen. He opened the app. Another series of numbers, different from the previous sender's but also attached to no domain name, had sent him a message with *Avalon Lake* in the subject line. He thought opening the email was probably a bad idea, but figured at the very least he would have something to add to his ever-expanding police report. Or maybe, he hoped, the email would contain some kind of lead on his brother. Though he recognized the chance of that happening as slim, he reasoned that he would never know unless he tried.

He opened the email and sighed with dismay when he saw the body filled with nothing but emoticons. Smiley faces. Smiley faces with devil horns. Ghosts. Aliens. Cats.

Hundreds of emoticons filled the message, but no words.

He scrolled all the way down and stopped at an attached file. He scanned the file for viruses and opened it. The file contained a series of photographs. The first photo showed a sign for a town called Avalon Lake. Black spray paint blocked out the population count and *zero* was tagged on top of the smudge in silver paint.

*Cute.*

He clicked on the next photo. An abandoned house. Lawn overgrown. A vehicle sat in the driveway, windows smashed out. A switchblade knife stuck out of the driver's side rear tire. Something dark smeared the concrete below. Oil. Or blood. Niles hoped it was oil.

Next photo. Another abandoned house. Similar state of disrepair.

Next. A street full of abandoned houses. Overgrown lawns. Vehicles parked on flat tires.

A shot of a lake, surrounded by woods. A sign read *Historic Avalon Lake. WE WHO SHALL NOT BE NAMED* spray painted over the decorative font. Niles thought something orange, fiery glowed beneath the water, but he couldn't tell for sure. The photo was old and grainy. Maybe a reflecting sunset, he thought.

Another photo. A dilapidated church, its courtyard cemetery overgrown with weeds and grass. Headstones hugged by tendrils of kudzu. Only shards remained of the stained glass windows.

Another picture showed the broadside of the same church. The phrase *WE WHO SHALL NOT BE NAMED* tagged the wall underneath a crude spray painted image of a bulbous, brain-like figure full of broken circuit boards and extending wiry tentacles.

He clicked through the rest of the photos, finding more of the same until one picture made him pause. A gray, late nineties model Ford Thunderbird. Parked in front of a rundown tin-roof warehouse. Back bumper adorned with several stickers. *I <3 TROMAVILLE HIGH SCHOOL. LEGALIZE IT. READ A DAMN BOOK! CONSENT IS ~~SEXY~~ REQUIRED.*

Leon's car. Leon's car was in Avalon Lake.

# 15

"I think I know where my brother is. A town called Avalon Lake. Have you heard of it?"

"I have not, sir. What makes you think he's there?"

The call taker had a young voice, with a valley girl slur.

"Someone emailed me pictures of the town. It's abandoned or something. His car was in one of them, parked on the street."

"And you're sure it's his car."

"One-hundred percent."

"Okay. I will forward that information to the detective."

"So, that's it?"

"Yeah, it's out of our jurisdiction, so the detective will have to work with whatever law enforcement agency oversees Avalon Lake."

"Right. Can I get the detective's name and number?"

"Of course, sir."

She provided the number. They disconnected. Niles dialed the detective's number. He got the answering machine. He left a message, made sure to exude annoyance with every word, and hung up. He returned to his computer. The email attachment still filled his screen. He scrolled until he came back to the photo of Leon's car. He opened another tab and searched for directions to Avalon Lake.

Ninety-three miles. An hour and a half drive, give or take.

"Fuck it," Niles said.

He got up from his desk chair, pulled on a pair of pants, and snatched his car keys from the kitchen counter. He went out to his car. Brought up directions to Avalon Lake on his phone. Drove out of his neighborhood and onto the main drag. Headed for Avalon Lake.

Toward Leon.

\*\*\*

Niles forced himself to chomp down a veggie burger. He nursed a thirty-two ounce coffee to keep himself sharp. He drove without music. Only the hum of the engine and the chatter of his thoughts kept him company.

Guilt gnawed at him. Its attack was two-pronged. He remembered masturbating to the *Smile* video, being unable to withhold his ecstasy, even in the face of violence. He remembered coming onto Leon's underage girlfriend in a drunken stupor. It felt as though something outside had overtaken him. Something old and primal and ugly. Something that awakened his darker tendencies and wrestled them out of his control.

The shame of his actions had physical weight. It made him slump in his driver's seat. He stared at the winding road ahead, numb and sedated.

He wondered what he would find in Avalon Lake. If he would find anything. It occurred to him that this could be some kind of a trap. He didn't care. He only cared about answers. If he found none in Avalon Lake, he would give up. But as long as he had hope, he had to move forward. No matter how vague that hope was.

He had his cell phone. If he found Leon's car, or if he got into trouble, he would just call 9-1-1. No reports. No case numbers. No unavailable detectives. Just emergency response from the police. No more fucking around.

A mile out from the abandoned town, on the side of an empty road, a sign of festive colors read *Harley's Arcade and Gasoline.* Niles pulled up to the pump and got out of his car. He slammed the rest of his coffee and chucked the empty cup in the nearest trashcan. He entered the building and approached the counter.

A twenty-five-year-old with shaggy blond hair and a sand-colored beard stood behind the counter. Games from the nineteen-eighties and nineties lined the walls. Cheap prizes filled a glass case under the counter. The employee grinned big and stupid when he saw Niles. Redness tinged the edges of his eyes. A stale marijuana smell hung in the air.

"Well, well, the first soul I've seen all day." The employee held out his hand. "Name's Harley. Nice to meet you."

Niles shook the extended hand. "Niles."

"Niles. Like *Frasier* and shit?"

"Yeah. Listen, I wonder if you can help me. I'm looking for my brother. About five-seven. Black hair passed his ears. Glasses. Drives a late nineties Ford Thunderbird."

Harley's eyes got big. "Don't think so. I mean, maybe. Hard to say."

"Right. Here's a picture." He brought out his phone and brought up a photograph of Leon and Dana outside the Austin capitol building.

Harley chewed his lip. His eyebrows scrunched into a frown. "Doesn't look familiar. Girl's pretty hot though. She missing too?"

Harley smirked. His words stung like barbs. Niles thought about reaching across the counter and taking the kid by the throat. He hadn't been in a physical confrontation since junior high school, but he didn't like Harley's attitude. Given his dark mindset since his father called him to tell him Leon had disappeared, little shits like Harley only served to incense him further.

He pushed the photograph deeper into Harley's personal space. "You're sure now?"

"Shit, man. You okay? Need to blow off some steam. Could give you a couple rounds of *Street Fighter II* on the house. Or are you more a *Mortal Kombat* guy?"

Niles withdrew his phone and put it back into his pocket. He took out his wallet and handed Harley a twenty.

"Just give me some gas."

"Whatever you say." Harley swiped the bill and Niles left the arcade.

After he filled up, he got back on the road. The sign for Avalon Lake loomed over him. The tagging showed a population of zero, just like in the photograph. He found it a lot less *cute* in person. It had an ominous quality. The sight of it put a lead ball in his stomach as he drove past.

He passed through a small stretch of forest and stopped when he reached Main Street. He got out of the car and glanced around. Shattered windows and graffiti-sprayed walls fronted every abandoned store. Several cars were parked along the street. Some had their windows smashed out. Others sat on deflated tires. One was stripped to its frame. The church from the photos stood at the street's opposite end.

Everything was quiet.

Niles pivoted and walked up to a pharmacy with its door hanging bent from its top hinge. He peered inside. Most of the shelves were empty. Several items were scattered across the floor, stuck in long-dried puddles of spilled soda. No signs of life. He checked inside other storefronts.

A dead gray cat lay on the floor of an empty barber shop, shears sticking out of its ribs. All the mirrors were shattered.

Flies congregated on the dirty furniture of an old frozen yogurt shop. The stink of curdled milk wafted out the windows and made Niles gag. The flies buzzed a hungry chorus.

Something heavy fell on Niles's shoulder.

# 16

Niles spun, lost his footing and dropped hard on his ass. Panic kicked in. The surprised jolted him bad enough, but being in a vulnerable position made it worse. His hands went up. He scrambled to find his footing.

"Hey, hey. Relax. I didn't mean to scare you." The voice was throaty, feminine and young. "What are you doing here?"

Niles stood and brushed dust from his pants. He gave the girl before him a once over. She wore a denim skirt over black leggings, and a black Iron Maiden shirt. Her hair was spiky and multicolored. A lip ring glinted at the side of her mouth. A camera dangled from a strap around her neck.

"Could ask you the same thing."

"I'm here on a dare. A bunch of my friends bet me I wouldn't go into the creepy ass church." She lifted the camera. "And, you know, pics or it didn't happen."

"Right."

She stuck out her hand. "I'm Temma."

"Niles." They shook. "Listen, do you know anything about this place?"

"I mean, a little. People just started gradually moving away some ten years ago. Some of them disappeared altogether. Eventually, there was no one left but squatters. Nowadays no one comes through at all, so there may not even be squatters left either. Of course everyone in the nearby towns thinks Avalon Lake is haunted."

"Of course."

"I don't believe in anything like that though. Guess that's

68

why I'm not afraid to take pictures of the spooky old church."

"Right. I'm headed that direction myself. Do you mind if I tag along?"

"Long as you're not a creeper, man."

"I'm not a creeper," he said, holding up his hand like he was taking an oath.

"Then sure, the more the merrier."

She spun and walked toward the church. He tried not to stare at her ass as it moved under the short skirt.

"So, you never did tell me what you're doing here," she said.

"My little brother went missing. I think he might be here." He told her about the email with the photos. He brought up the image of his brother's car and showed it to her. "You know where this place is?"

She shook her head. "Sorry. Any idea *why* your brother would have ended up here?"

"Wish I knew." He told her about Leon and Shiloh's exploration of the deep web and how they had stumbled upon photos of an abandoned town, a town he now believed was Avalon Lake. He told her about the message they'd received. "You're sure no one lives here?"

"Like I said, there may still be some squatters left, but I don't know. Feels pretty empty right now, if you ask me."

He glanced around. They stopped in front of the church stairs. The red door hung ajar, its paint faded and peeled from years exposed to the elements. Holes were kicked in the lower panels. Vines clung to the stone walls. Skeletal remains of a large rodent lay across the top step. Dry ragged skin hung from its rib bones.

"I know what you mean."

Temma smirked and gestured at the door. "Well, you first."

"I thought you said you weren't afraid."

"You saying you are?"

"Guess not."

"Good. We'll go in together. Besides," she gave her right boot a kick, "I've got a knife in here. I'll protect us."

He nodded and shuffled to her side. They ascended the stairs, stepped over the rodent carcass, and stopped when they reached the red door. He reached for the handle, the brass hot under the sunlight. He winced and withdrew his hand. Temma reached inside the cracked door and pulled. Its rusty hinges moaned as it opened outward. An earthy smell came from inside, underneath that, the smell of wet ink.

All the pews were overturned, some of them split and splintered. Nature had reclaimed most of the space. Vines from the exterior wall sprawled through broken stained glass windows, clinging to the wall and spilling across the floor. Cobwebs dangled from every corner of the ceiling. Black mold formed grotesque shapes along the walls. The door to the rectory had been removed and the opening revealed a pile of broken, old electronic equipment.

His eyes flitted to the opposite end of the chapel. The crucified savior had lost his head. A bulky computer monitor rested on his shoulders, its screen dark. One arm had been snapped off. Wires entangled the stump, wrapped around the corresponding limb of the cross. Zeroes and ones and unrecognizable glyphs tattooed Christ's chest, arm, and legs. A keyboard with some of the letters missing had been nailed to his midsection. Someone had strapped a purple dildo to his plastic loincloth.

The altar lay split in two. Between the severed halves stood a large printer-fax machine combination. Several sheets of dot matrix paper were stacked on top. Niles went to exchange glances with Temma. She already had her camera out and aimed at the altar.

"Aren't you the least bit freaked out?" he asked.

She shrugged. "Maybe a little. Still need to get these pictures though."

She stepped forward and he followed, careful not to trip over any vines. Wires and cables were entwined with the foliage. Niles tapped Temma's shoulder.

"Look." He pointed to the floor.

"What the hell?" She crouched and took one of the thick cables in her hand. "Weird."

The wires and vines were braided together in places. In others, they were indistinguishable. Meshed together like some kind of hybrid plant. She let the cable fall, and took a series of photos. They proceeded toward the altar.

Niles approached the stack of dot matrix paper and lifted the first sheet.

Temma read over his shoulder. "The following is the testament of We Who Shall Not Be Named."

"Weird."

"I'll say."

Niles flipped through more pages. He recognized some passages as Bible verses, mostly from the Old Testament, some from Revelation. Other passages read like something out of H.P. Lovecraft. Talk of old gods, and hideous, unutterable blasphemies. On another page: *Death, tamed, went in front of me at each corner offering me his hand nicely, and sometimes lay on the ground with a noise of creaking jaws giving me velvet glances from the bottom of puddles.* And, positioned beneath it: *Time and Space died yesterday. We are already living in the absolute.* At the bottom of the page: *We want to glorify war — the only cure for the world — militarism, patriotism, the destructive gesture of the anarchists, the beautiful ideas which kill, and contempt for woman.*

"Those," Temma said. "Those are from the *Futurist Manifesto*."

Niles turned the page. Lines of code filled the next sheet.
"Any idea what that means?"
"No clue."
The printer whined to life. Paper shuffled. Something beeped. The printer spit out a sheet of paper. Niles and Temma exchanged glances. Temma's eyes were wide. Her lips pressed together. She shrugged. Niles reached for the sheet.

*WELCOME, NILES WELCOME, TEMMA*
*WE HOPE U ENJOY UR STAY...*
*...IN HELL LULZ* ☺☺☺ *666 LULZZZZZZZZZ*
*BET U LOVE PURPLE JEEZUS COCK*
*UR GONNA FUCKING DIE HERE CUNTZ*
*C U SOON*

# 17

"We seriously need to go," Temma said when they got outside the church.

"I agree, but first I need to see if my brother's car is here. We've only seen Main Street."

"Fuck your brother's car. Motherfuckers here want to kill us."

"Yeah, but…"

"Look, you can stay if you want, but I'm making myself scarce." She turned and started walking.

"Temma, wait. You're not going to get far on foot."

"Well, I'm not sticking around."

He sighed. She was right. Something was seriously wrong here. Staying here was a terrible idea. Coming here to begin with didn't top the list of the smartest things he had done either.

"Okay, okay," he said. "Wait up."

They retraced their steps back up Main Street. They glanced over their shoulders the entire way, paranoia and panic increasing with every step. When they reached the vehicle, Niles froze in his tracks.

"You've got to be fucking kidding me," he said.

Temma saw what he saw. "Oh, shit."

The tires sat deflated under his Corolla. Niles walked around the car to confirm. All four of them. He slammed his fist against the back panel. Pain throbbed in his wrist.

"Fuck."

"You have a spare?" she asked.

"I don't have four fucking spares."

She cringed. "You're right, sorry."

"No, don't be. It's been a bullshit day." He shook his head. Exhaustion weighed down his limbs and muddied his thoughts.

"Do you...want me to call someone?"

"What? Uh, yeah, good idea." She pulled out her phone and wrinkled her brow. "What is it?"

She lifted her phone up to show him. A yellow smiley face sat in the middle of the screen, blocking her icons, black eyes staring. Niles reached for his phone. The same emoticon floated on his monitor. He tapped the screen. The smile became an O of surprise and the cheeks flushed pink. The smile and yellow color returned as soon as Niles withdrew his finger. His mouth went dry. Dread settled in the pit of his stomach.

"This is bad," Temma said.

He tended to agree, but tried to keep calm. "Look, we'll just...we'll just walk until we find someone who can help us. There's that arcade up the road. They should have a phone."

"Harley's?"

"Uh huh."

"Oh, okay." She sounded weak, tired, the way Niles felt.

They started walking past Niles's car. He put his arm around her shoulders, but she shook him off.

"I'm fine."

"Sorry," he said and stuffed his hand in his pocket.

Something creaked behind them. It sounded like the trunk to his car. Niles turned. The figure emerging from his trunk was dressed in a tight gray outfit that covered their entire body, and a red devil mask with curving horns, black eyes, and a fang-baring smile. Their hands clutched a length of metal pipe. The figure barreled toward them.

"Temma, run." She turned to see what Niles saw, toward the pounding, approaching footsteps, and yelped. "Go!"

74

She sprang into a sprint. Niles turned to do the same, but the masked assailant was too close. The pipe swung, struck Niles's skull with a metallic thud, and everything went black.

# 18

Temma's feet slammed pavement. Her breath stung as it tore down her throat and into her lungs. She dropped her backpack to reduce her weight. She reached her max speed and exceeded it. Part of her wanted to look back and check on Niles, but she'd heard the impact of metal against flesh, the crumple of his body collapsing. She feared the worst. A more selfish side of her, an animal instinct of self-preservation hoped the attacker would be too busy with Niles to pursue her. Her sense of panic and need to survive far eclipsed any inkling of guilt.

The edge of town loomed ahead, over the crest of the hill. Of course, she could be pursued beyond the town limits, but they represented a symbolic freedom. She could reach the main road and flag down help. Or run into McCool's and use the phone. She just had to go a little farther.

Something hit her from the side, knocking the wind out of her, pushing her off her feet. Her elbow, shoulder and hip struck pavement. Loose gravel gouged her skin through her clothes. The heavy force that hit her pinned her to the street, as her body tried to make sense of what happened.

Another figure wearing gray nylon lay on top of her, an enlarged skull mask hiding his features. His hands found their way around her throat. She gasped for air, already having so little left in her lungs after the tackle. She squirmed and kicked, but the hands around her neck tightened. Her assailant had too much body weight pressed against her small frame for her to get much leverage. She dug her nails into the attacker's sides and raked his skin. He cried out and loosened his grip.

Temma rammed her forehead into the mask. The plaster cracked. Something soft gave way. He cried out again, this time at a higher pitch. She thought she bloodied his nose. He rolled over and she crawled out from under him, made it to her feet. A hand closed around her ankle, sent her tumbling forward. Her chin scraped the pavement and she bit her tongue. Fatigue set in, drowning out any remaining adrenaline. She screamed for help once, before the assailant climbed on her back and slammed her face into the ground.

# 19

Someone was sobbing. Niles tried to crane his neck to view the source of the sounds and the pain blinded him. He shut his eyes and waited for the agony to pass. When he opened them, he tried to survey his surroundings. Some kind of warehouse, overgrown with weeds and littered with computer equipment. More sobbing. He turned his head again, this time exercising more caution. The pain still made him wince, but his slower movement made it manageable.

Temma sat beside him, arms and legs tied to a chair, tears running in dirty streams down her cheeks. A large gash on the side of her head had crusted her sandy hair with blood.

"Where are we?" he asked, the act of speaking sending him into a coughing fit.

"I…I don't know…I just…I want to go home."

Niles's heart ached for her. She was still a kid, no more than sixteen. Had her whole life ahead of her. Probably hadn't even lost her virginity yet. He didn't expect either of them to make it through the rest of the day. He had researched enough real life crimes to know that these sorts of stories seldom had happy endings.

He tried to move closer to her, to power through the pain and offer some sort of comfort, but he found he, too, had been tied to a chair.

"We gotta…we gotta scream for help," he said. She whimpered. "Come on, you can do it. *Help! Someone please! Get us the fuck out of here!*"

Temma echoed his pleas. She jerked herself back and forth in her chair. Niles followed suit. The chair didn't feel particularly sturdy. Maybe he could break it. He shifted his weight, kept on screaming. Their cries formed a desperate chorus, one that reverberated off the cracked concrete floor, echoed off the tin roof, traveled through the broken windows and into the surrounding woods. Some birds cawed in response. Others flew away from the abrasive cries.

Niles tried to catch his breath.

"What are we gonna do?" Temma asked.

He tried to think. Instinctively, he bit his lip, and exacerbated an undiscovered wound. The scab tore free, blood teased his taste buds, and he winced.

"Shit," he said.

"Wait."

"What?"

"My knife. It's still in my boot."

"Can you get to it?"

"I can try."

She teetered side to side. She tried wiggling her right leg free.

Footsteps plodded somewhere in the nearby woods. Someone coming.

"*Help us! Please, I know you're out there!*" Temma stopped.

"Keep trying," Niles said and resumed yelling for help.

Temma tipped her chair to the left and fell to the floor. Outside, the footsteps drew closer. Niles didn't expect someone coming to help them, but kept hollering in vain hope. Vain hope that the approaching people weren't their kidnappers. The buckle on one of Temma's boots caught on the leg of the chair. She tried yanking her foot free. She grinded her teeth and groaned with exertion.

The door flung open. A bloated, pale shape stood limp in the doorway. It was wrapped in wires and had too many limbs dangling from its bulbous, patchwork torso. The figure radiated the pungent stink of decay. Niles counted three eyeless heads, stitched across the creature's chest. One of the heads belonged to Leon.

This was a creature of nightmares. Niles didn't believe in supernatural monsters. In his years of research, he knew all too well the cruelty of humanity. He believed any stories of otherworldly entities committing acts of terror softened the blow. It was easier than believing your fellow man capable of atrocity. Yet, here was a beast, not of this world and looming before him.

It lurched forward, through the threshold. Niles squirmed in his seat. He tried to scream, but could make no sounds. Beside him, Temma's boot scraped the chair leg, but he barely heard it. The monster held his attention. Leon's empty eye sockets and lolling black tongue kept him entranced.

The creature passed stacks of broken down electronics. Wires and ruined flesh dragged across the floor with every step. The creature stopped at the top of the stairs, leading down into warehouse's main floor. And fell forward.

Niles's stomach lurched with every wet thud. Every crack of bone. Every squish of a leaky organ. The creature lay in a mangled heap, crumpled and unmoving. Dark fluid pooled around its slimy edges.

Two men stood at the top of the stairs wearing masks. The Devil who had jumped them on Main was joined by a man wearing an enlarged skull over his head. They both held leashes. Devil had his clenched in his right hand. Skull held his in his left. The men walked forward, dragging the leashes behind them. A naked woman crawled on the end of each leash. Their heads hung, as if ashamed. Bruises and cuts marked their bodies. The masked men and their women flanked the monstrosity at the foot of the stairs. Boots, and bare hands and knees stuck in the pooling fluids.

The man in the devil mask turned toward Temma. The

blade lay on the floor, free of its ankle sheath. She attempted to shift her chair so that her hands could reach the knife. Skull turned to watch. The women did likewise. One of them smiled, revealing broken teeth sitting jagged in her bruised jaw. Niles thought of the *Smile* video. Thought this might be the same woman.

Niles rocked in his chair. The legs creaked as they wobbled. Maybe he could get free.

Temma's chair squeaked against the floor. She moved an inch at a time. She winced and groaned as her shoulder scraped concrete. The masked figures and their women just watched. They waited until she reached the knife, and the Devil stepped forward and kicked stomped on her fingers. She shrieked. Niles whimpered as the Devil kicked the knife aside, into a pile of moldy keyboards.

"Why are you doing this? What the fuck is wrong with you?"

The words fell from Niles's lips, even ask he knew the futility of asking such questions. People like this didn't need a reason do what they did. It was brutality for the sake of brutality. It came from an inability to see people as anything other than objects. They felt a weaker person deserved to be abused. It was a twisted, Darwinian narrative. They were schoolyard bullies, only cranked up to eleven.

*But that darkness lives in me too, doesn't it?*

*It's the same darkness that drives me get off to a scene of degradation.*

*To try and fuck my missing brother's underage girlfriend.*

*To isolate myself from my wife when she needed me most.*

*It's a disease.*

*And we all have it.*

The Devil drove his heel deeper into Temma's fingers. Her cries punctuated the sickening cracks of her bones. Devil reared back and kicked her in the stomach. The blow drove the wind from her, rendered her screams wet gasps.

*We have it in varying levels of severity.*

*But it's the same ugly disease.*

*The same darkness.*

*I recognize this, yet I want to live.*

Niles fidgeted. The right front chair leg bent and creaked. He dared to hope.

Someone hit him. His vision went white. His wrists screamed as he fell backwards and crushed them under his body weight, as the back of the chair dug into his forearms.

The tin roof hung above him, indifferent and cold. Skull straddled him, leaned down and drove a succession of fists into his face. Niles gagged on blood. He tried to squirm free, bound to the chair, pinned by the larger man. He started to choke as thick iron-rich clots ran down his throat.

Skull dismounted and kicked Niles on his side. The chair rolled and cracked. Splinters drove into Niles's arms. The chair had weakened considerably. He could probably break it if he had enough strength left. He was facing Temma. Devil crawled off of her, finished dealing his own round of beatings. Devil and Skull returned to their places beside the oozing monstrosity. Some of the electronic equipment beeped and shifted, turning itself on.

"*Let us go. Let us go. Let us fucking go,*" Temma whispered over and over, drooling a string of blood and snot.

Devil and Skull exchanged glances, their expressions unreadable behind their masks. They reached into their pants and each produced a flogger. In a synchronized motion, they swung the floggers at the women's pale bare asses. Twin wet snaps reverberated through the warehouse. The women flinched on impact. The strikes forced their mouths open, showing the jagged broken teeth. One of them moaned. Niles couldn't tell if it was in pleasure or pain. The women crawled forward as their masters unhanded their leashes.

"Please, help us," Temma said between ragged breaths.

Devil's woman squatted on top of Temma's face. Skull's woman hovered above Niles's. Her cunt was raw and red. Her ass covered in welts. Niles tried to squirm out from under her. The urine sprayed him in the face. Hot on his skin, the liquid stung his eyes. He tried to turn away, but it only resulted in another part of his face getting wet. It soaked his hair and stung his eyes. Tasted bitter as it seeped through his lips. He thought he heard another pattering of piss from where the Devil's woman squatted over Temma. The women finished peeing and returned to their masters, kneeling again in the oozy puddle.

The machines continued to beep and blink. The pile shook and pulsed, as if large rats crawled beneath all the clutter.

More masked figures entered. A pig. A pumpkin. Someone in a Jason Voorhees mask. Jason carried an old stereo and set it in front of the bloated form. He pressed a button and stepped back.

The tape began with a hiss of static. Low-pitched distorted voices chanted in hushed tones. A minor-key melody played along with the voices, repetitive and haunting. It sounded like something he wasn't supposed to be listening to, something inspired by depravity, something diabolical. The idea of evil music was ridiculous, of course, but he couldn't stifle the dread the notes stirred. He wanted to reach out and take Temma's hand, but his wrists remained tied, pinned beneath him and the chair.

The naked women lowered their heads. Their hair fell like knotty curtains over their faces. All the masked men raised their arms. The sounds on the tape increased in volume, even the static, which sizzled above everything, allowing only pieces of the melody and the voices to filter through. Equipment around the room expanded and contracted with breath, their material becoming soft, *organic*.

"Oh, what the fuck?" Niles said.

He shifted side to side. He tried lifting himself and falling back. Pieces of the chair splintered as its frame creaked and bent. The masked figures and their women were too entranced with their ritual to notice. Niles tried to focus only on getting free, but as he wriggled, his gaze remained fixed on the electronic equipment coming to life. Coming to *bioorganic* life. Becoming *flesh*.

*And maybe more than flesh.*

*It's responding to the ritual.*

*The prayer.*

*That's stupid,* he thought, even as panic gripped him. As unbelievable as the phenomenon was, there had to be a logical, science-based explanation. But he didn't think much about that. He only dwelt on the fear, and it fueled him as he struggled to get free.

Something fiery glowed beneath the pile of broken down electronics. Niles thought it might be fire, at first, and Temma echoed his thoughts.

*"They're gonna fucking burn us the fuck alive!"*

But the glowing substance had a liquid quality, resembling viscous magma more than fire. It leaked through the gaps in the cluttered electronics

The stereo was blaring now. The static filled Niles's skull. The chants echoed off the tin roof and concrete floor.

Wires sprawled out from the pile of equipment and lashed at the floor, striking sparks. Computer monitors and televisions switched on, displaying green code and glyphs. The items began to meld with the growing blob. The hooded figures chanted along with the voices on the tape. Static grew deafening.

More wires encircled the bulbous shape between the masked figures. Magma mixed with pus. The monstrosity rose, wires and strips of wet flesh dangling. Eyes opened on the three severed heads, black as camera lenses. Thick cables lolled from each mouth in place of tongues. Blue lightning surged through the orange blob, through the pale monstrosity. The amorphous shape spread across the floor like spilled batter. Thick, sinewy tentacles wormed toward Niles. Sparking white and bleeding black. Twisting and thickening.

The masked figures and women remained in position, even as the creature grew and pulsed around them. A ragged hole opened, somewhere near the creature's center, full of jagged plastic, glass and metal. *The mouth of Satan.*

Something heavy fell upon Niles. He was pushed onto his side. Fresh pain flared in his right arm, crushed under the chair and pricked by splinters. Something pulled at the ropes on his wrist. He glanced over his shoulder.

Temma. Somehow she'd gotten free. She was sawing through the ropes with her knife. Soon she would free him. The tendrils snaked closer to them.

"Hurry," he said.

"Trying."

The ropes gave and loosened. His hands came free. They were inches from the monster's reach. Temma helped lift the chair so he could get his right arm out. They untied his feet together. He rose to run away, but the tendril encircled his ankle, sent him face first to the floor. Milkweed leaves stabbed at his forehead. Dirt clouded his nostrils and stung his eyes.

Temma helped him to his feet, but the tentacle would not let go. It was too strong. More of the appendages darted forward, ensnared Temma's left arm. She cried out and tried stabbing the creature. The knife drew strange, multicolored blood, but seemed to have little effect on the monster. The tentacle holding Niles's ankle let go and took hold of

Temma's leg, wrapping itself all the way up to her thigh.

Niles stumbled backwards. He almost lost his footing again, tripping over a crack in the floor. He steadied himself and lifted his gaze. Temma was enshrouded in orange and black. Only her head, the hand holding the knife, and her left leg were visible. She was screaming, her eyes expressing abject terror.

She released the knife and reached for Niles. She cried for him to help her. Niles remained frozen to the spot. Something tight clenched his belly. He felt pulled in two directions. Toward her and toward the nearest window. More tendrils wormed across the walls and ceiling, across the floor. Temma was being pulled toward the awful mouth of the beast. Toward its mechanical, gnashing jaws.

Niles turned and ran. *Too late for her. It's too damn late.*

"You bastard," she shrieked after him. "*You son of a bitch!*"

He stopped at a broken window, where a low tree branch had grown to reach inside the warehouse. He cast one last look at Temma, her face purple and twisted into a snarl. The tentacles lifted her, fed her feet first into the jaws. The mouth bit into her calves. All the anger leeched from her voice, replaced by cries of sheer agony. Blood sprayed from the wounds like water from a hose with many punctures. Niles turned away as the jaws clamped down again, shattering her kneecaps with gritty, wet chewing sounds. Niles climbed out the window, shards of glass scraping his forearms and torso. He slipped through the window and fell to the forest floor. Temma's screams tore through the static and garbled chants; they tore through everything.

# 20

Niles ran, feet pumping faster than he could think, faster than he could breathe. He swayed, wobbled, and staggered, somehow keeping his feet, despite the pain and disorienting panic. He didn't dare look back at the warehouse, toward the lurching clatter of the hardware creature, toward the sizzles and chirps of broken down electronics, toward Temma's shrill, agonized screams.

Paranoia made his eyes dart side to side. He fully expected a masked assailant to come from behind a tree and knock him silly with a lead pipe. He hadn't bothered to find a true path from the warehouse. He tromped through underbrush, jutting roots and rocks, and prayed he didn't trip on something.

A wet choking sound cut off Temma's screams.

*My fault. I left her to die.*

The thought slipped through his frantic mind static and tugged at his conscience. His steps began to slow. His guts sank.

*No. Keep running. There's nothing you could have done. Nothing you can do now.*

The moment's hesitation ended when the door to the warehouse opened and slammed shut behind him. Someone was in pursuit. Niles quickened his pace. Pushed aside low-hanging branches. Trudged through a pile of fallen pine needles.

He reached an embankment and climbed. He fell, crawled on all fours for several paces before forcing himself back to his feet. Behind him, the pursuing footsteps drew closer. He heard only one set and paused to risk a look back. The man in the Jason mask ascended the embankment, clutching a knife with a curved blade.

Niles scanned the ground for some kind of weapon. He settled on a jagged stone and hurled it at his pursuer. The rock struck Jason in the ribs and he groaned and stopped to press his hand to the affected area. Niles turned and resumed his racing exodus. He reached the top of the embankment and a break in the woods. The empty street lay before him.

Jason scrambled up behind Niles. Niles lifted another stone, this one much larger and requiring both hands, and hurled it down at his attacker. The stone nailed Jason in the chest and sent him spilling down the embankment and into a stump. Niles zeroed in on the knife. He would need a weapon if anyone else in town was waiting for the right moment to ambush him. He bounded down the hill.

The injured Jason stirred against the stump, tried to rise and fell backward. Flecks of blood spattered through the mask's breathing holes. Niles lifted the mask, revealing the face of a boy no more than Leon's age. For a brief moment, Niles pitied him, thought maybe Jason was just a regular kid who fell in with the wrong crowd, but the memory Leon's eviscerated form, dancing on marionette strings brought a surge of grief-fueled rage. Niles kicked Jason in the forehead over and over, the back of the boy's head striking the stump and making a bloody imprint. The surface meeting Niles's boot got softer, looser. Something cracked, then squished. Niles removed the toe of his boot, pulling hunks of brain and chips of skull with it. Jason's face had been reduced to a red, ragged mess.

Niles tried to collect himself. His breath tore in and out. His gorge rose, forcing him to dry heave. He put his hands on his knees and closed his eyes. He tried to tell himself killing Jason had been necessary, that it would have come down to him or the knife wielding boy, but he wasn't convinced. *I didn't have to run back down the hill and kick his fucking skull in.* But the violence felt good, *honest*, and maybe that was what troubled him most of all. He bent and swiped the knife from Jason's still-twitching hand.

# 21

Passing through the rest of the town proved easier than Niles expected. He slowed his pace to a staggering shuffle, but still had yet to catch his breath. No one jumped out of any houses or abandoned cars wielding lead pipes, but still he kept the knife clutched tight and at the ready, still he stayed hyper alert, checking over his shoulders at every intersection, at every unexpected sound. He reached his car, all four tires deflated with defeat, the trunk still open from when Devil came out swinging.

The ground trembled. He froze in place, too exhausted to panic.

"Oh, what the fuck now?"

He looked back toward the woods, toward the warehouse he escaped, toward the lake full of infinite mystery. Red-orange light shone between the trees. It reminded him of an explosion, but other than the shaky ground, no concussion accompanied the flash. The fiery light obscured the trees, became a pulsing red dome. And then it was gone.

Niles felt dizzy. He stuck out his hands to balance himself. Held the knife point as far from his body as possible. When his equilibrium returned, he blinked several times, turned and walked back toward the town limits.

No cars passed him on the main drag. The crazy thought crossed his mind that he was the only person left in the world, but the notion didn't seem so crazy. The world had new rules now. The veil had been torn down and the illusion of a stable reality no longer existed.

He halted his steps some twenty-five paces from Harley's

Arcade. The hot pink retro brush font on the business sign stood before him like an oasis. He stared. He thought the ground was trembling again, but discovered the tremors came from his own limbs. His gaze flashed to the knife in his hand. If Harley saw the weapon, he'd more likely shoot Niles than call for help. The fact Niles was covered in blood wouldn't do much to help his cause either. Niles let the knife fall with a metallic clink against the pavement and shuffled to the arcade entrance.

Inside, the games beeped and chirped. Eight-bit music played over the PA. Smells of old plastic and cheap cleaner made his nostrils itch. The arcade was empty. Niles's lips quivered.

"H-hello?" he said.

He tiptoed farther into the business, past pinball machines and vintage fighting games and miniature basketball courts with worn netting and red digital shot clocks stopped at double zero. He approached the counter and scanned his surroundings.

"Harley, you in here?"

Something slid across the floor. A door opening. Maybe.

Footsteps approached, sounded like they were coming up from somewhere downstairs. Niles tensed. A second door opened just behind the counter. A shaped emerged, greasy black hair obscuring the face, wiping pale hands on the front of a dirty shirt.

"Sorry, man. I was in the shitter. Sometimes forget to lock up being so off-the-beaten…" Harley raised his head. "Holy fuck, man. What happened to you?"

Niles said nothing.

"You just come from Avalon Lake? Man, I tell people not to go messing around in there. Town's abandoned, but whole bunch of weirdoes is usually squatting there."

Niles opened his mouth. He croaked out an extended,

single syllable, but couldn't form a word. Harley glanced over Niles and blinked behind thick lensed glasses.

"Hey, man, is that blood? You're not a psycho or something, are you?"

Niles shook his head.

"All right, all right, let me…" He raised a finger as if telling Niles to hold on for one minute. "Let me call you some help."

Niles nodded. Harley stepped to the side of the counter. He reached down and ruffled through some items Niles couldn't see. Niles wanted to scream for Harley to hurry, but he was too exhausted to speak, maybe even in shock.

He thought about Bella. Thought maybe he should call her when he gets back home. While he feared what life would be like now that the veil had been torn all the way down, feared that he would never be able to see the world outside of this new post-traumatic lens, he also felt an intense need to reconnect with the people in life who meant something to him. The trauma of losing Simon had driven him and Bella apart, when it should have brought them together. Now, more than ever, he wanted to lean on her, to repair the rift. If she hadn't already moved on, Niles hoped she would feel the same way.

A slide and a click drew him out of his thoughts. He dialed in on the gray firearm in Harley's hand.

"Why?" he said.

The gun fired. His knee disintegrated in a cloud of red. The pain sent him crashing to the floor. Harley stepped out from behind the counter and stood over Niles, gun aimed, ready to put a slug in Niles's chest.

"Sorry, man, it's nothing personal. It's just…" He giggled. "Well, it's not business either. Call it a philosophy."

Outside, a car was pulling up.

"Please…just…let me go. I won't tell anyone you shot me."

"No can do, man."

The car came to a stop. Niles knew better than to call for help. He bet whoever sat behind the wheel of that vehicle had ties to Avalon Lake, to the people who killed Leon and Temma, to that monster in the warehouse. Someone got out of the car and entered the arcade. Something metal dragged on the floor behind the driver. Niles tried to look and see who was approaching.

The man in the devil mask stopped less than five paces from where Niles lay and lifted the metal pipe. He held it across his chest with both hands. His heavy breathing rasped beneath the mask. Black eye holes gazed down at Niles.

"There are others like us," Harley said. "Decentralized cells of bored, perverted mother fuckers looking for something to get invested in, so long as we can act behind the scenes. Other old gods, like the one from the lake, looking for twisted weirdoes like us to give them new life. The dark web gives us a home and the gods a doorway into our world. Teaches them new shit. Tell you the truth, sometimes I don't know who corrupted who. Fucking beautiful, you think about it. You get to be a part of that. Fucking cool, right?"

"Fuck you," Niles said.

Harley smirked, exchanged a glance with Devil. "Me or you, bro?"

Devil raised the pipe. Niles screamed once. The pipe fell again and again.

**Lucas Mangum** is the author of Flesh and Fire, Mania, Engines of Ruin, and Gods of the Dark Web. He currently resides in Austin, TX with his family, but can also be found on Twitter @LMangumFiction. Feel free to follow him there and engage him in conversations about horror movies and prowrestling.

# deadite press

**"Earthworm Gods" Brian Keene -** One day, it starts raining-and never stops. Global super-storms decimate the planet, eradicating most of mankind. Pockets of survivors gather on mountaintops, watching as the waters climb higher and higher. But as the tides rise, something else is rising, too. Now, in the midst of an ecological nightmare, the remnants of humanity face a new menace, in a battle that stretches from the rooftops of submerged cities to the mountaintop islands jutting from the sea. The old gods are dead. Now is the time of the Earthworm Gods...

**"The Complex" Brian Keene -** There was no warning. No chance to escape. They came suddenly. Naked. Bloodthirsty. Sadistic. They descended upon the Pine Village Apartment Complex, relentlessly torturing and killing anyone they could find. Fearing for their lives, the residents of the complex must band together. Eleven strangers. The only thing they have in common is the unstoppable horde that wants to kill them. If they are to make it through the night, they must fight back.

**"An Occurrence in Crazy Bear Valley" Brian Keene-** The Old West has never been weirder or wilder than it has in the hands of master horror writer Brian Keene. Morgan and his gang are on the run--from their pasts and from the posse riding hot on their heels, intent on seeing them hang. But when they take refuge in Crazy Bear Valley, their flight becomes a siege as they find themselves battling a legendary race of monstrous, bloodthirsty beings. Now, Morgan and his gang aren't worried about hanging. They just want to live to see the dawn.

**"Entombed II" Brian Keene-** It has been several months since the disease known as Hamelin's Revenge decimated the world. Civilization has collapsed and the dead far outnumber the living. The survivors seek refuge from the roaming zombie hordes, but one-by-one, those shelters are falling.Twenty-five survivors barricade themselves inside a former military bunker buried deep beneath a luxury hotel. They are safe from the zombies...but are they safe from one another?

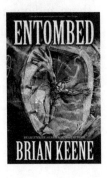

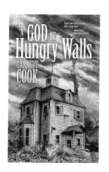

**"A God of Hungry Walls" Garrett Cook** - When you are within my walls, I am God. I have always been here and I will always be. I have complete dominion. I control what you see, what you feel, and how you think. I will bend reality to whatever I wish. I will show you your worst fears and make you indulge in your darkest desires. Your pain is my pleasure. Your tears are my ambrosia. Your despair is my joy. I will break you. I will ruin you. Once you enter me, there is no escape. I will own you, forever.

**"The Lucky Ones Died First" Jack Bantry** - Crushed heads, entrails, and piles of body parts are littering the woods surrounding the quaint English vacation town of Hambleton. A hungry cryptid is on the loose and is biting and tearing to pieces whoever and whatever it can catch. Now the residents must team up with a former-Nazi Bigfoot hunter to save themselves and their livelihood from this monstrous horror. People must fight. Many of them will not live to see the next day…

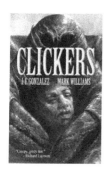

**"Clickers" J. F. Gonzalez and Mark Williams-** They are the Clickers, giant venomous blood-thirsty crabs from the depths of the sea. The only warning to their rampage of dismemberment and death is the terrible clicking of their claws. But these monsters aren't merely here to ravage and pillage. They are being driven onto land by fear. Something is hunting the Clickers. Something ancient and without mercy. *Clickers* is J. F. Gonzalez and Mark Williams' gore-soaked cult classic tribute to the giant monster B-movies of yesteryear.

**"Spermjackers from Hell" Christine Morgan** - Let's summon a succubus, they said. It'll be fun, they said…We were wrong. Really fucking wrong. The demon is not what we thought and it's making horrible things happen. People are cutting into each other's junk, some guy is fucking his dog, and sex slugs from Hell are raping us and stealing our semen in order to build a goddamn hive! We didn't mean for any of this. But we're gonna fix it… Just after a few more beers and bong hits.

**AVAILABLE FROM AMAZON.COM**

# deadite press

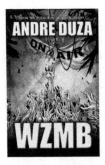

**"WZMB" Andre Duza** - It's the end of the world, but we're not going off the air! Martin Stone was a popular shock jock radio host before the zombie apocalypse. Then for six months the dead destroyed society. Humanity is now slowly rebuilding and Martin Stone is back to doing what he does best-taking to the airwaves. Host of the only radio show in this new world, he helps organize other survivors. But zombies aren't the only threat. There are others that thought humanity needed to end.

**"Tribesmen" Adam Cesare** - Thirty years ago, cynical sleazeball director Tito Bronze took a tiny cast and crew to a desolate island. His goal: to exploit the local tribes, spray some guts around, cash in on the gore-spattered 80s Italian cannibal craze. But the pissed-off spirits of the island had other ideas. And before long, guts were squirting behind the scenes, as well. While the camera kept rolling...

**"Reincarnage" Ryan Harding and Jason Taverner** - In the 80's a supernatural killer known as Agent Orange terrorized the United States. No matter how many times he was killed, he kept coming back to spread death and mayhem. With no other choice, the government walled off the small town, woods, and lake that Agent Orange used as his hunting ground. This seemed to contain the killer and his killing sprees ended. Or so the populace thought...

**"Suffer the Flesh" Monica J. O'Rourke** - Zoey always wished she was thinner. One day she meets a strange woman who informs her of an ultimate weight-loss program, and Zoey is quickly abducted off the streets of Manhattan and forced into this program. Zoey's enrolling whether she wants to or not. Held hostage with many other women, Zoey is forced into degrading acts of perversion for the amusement of her captors. ...

**"Answers of Silence" Geoff Cooper** - Deadite Press is proud to present the extremely sought after horror stories of Geoff Cooper. Collecting fifteen tales of the weird, the horrific, and the strange. Fans of Brian Keene, Jack Ketchum, and Bryan Smith won't want to miss this collection from one of the unsung masters of modern horror. You won't forget your visit to Geoff Cooper's dark and deranged world.

**"Boot Boys of the Wolf Reich" David Agranoff** - PIt is the summer of 1989 and they spend their days hanging out and having fun, and their nights fighting the local neo-Nazi gangs. Driven back and badly beaten, the local Nazi contingent finds the strangest of allies - The last survivor of a cult of Nazi werewolf assassins. An army of neo-Nazi werewolves are just what he needs. But first, they have some payback for all those meddling Anti-racist SHARPs...

**"White Trash Gothic" Edward Lee** - Luntville is not just some bumfuck town in the sticks. It is a place where the locals make extra cash by filming necro porn, a place where vigilantes practice a horrifying form of justice they call dead-dickin', a place haunted by the ghosts of serial killers, occult demons, and a monster called the Bighead. And as the writer attempts to make sense of the town and his connection to it, he will be challenged in ways that test the very limit of his sanity.

**"Whargoul" Dave Brockie** - It is a beast born in bullets and shrapnel, feeding off of pain, misery, and hard drugs. Cursed to wander the Earth without the hope of death, it is reborn again and again to spread the gospel of hate, abuse, and genocide. But what if it's not the only monster out there? What if there's something worse? From Dave Brockie, the twisted genius behind GWAR, comes a novel about the darkest days of the twentieth century.

## AVAILABLE FROM AMAZON.COM

# deadite press

**"Header" Edward Lee** - In the dark backwoods, where law enforcement doesn't dare tread, there exists a special type of revenge. Something so awful that it is only whispered about. Something so terrible that few believe it is real. Stewart Cummings is a government agent whose life is going to Hell. His wife is ill and to pay for her medication he turns to bootlegging. But things will get much worse when bodies begin showing up in his sleepy small town. Victims of an act known only as "a Header."

**"Punk Rock Ghost Story" David Agranoff** - In the summer of 1982, legendary Indianapolis hardcore band, The Fuckers, became the victim of a mysterious tragedy. They returned home without their vocalist and the band disappeared. A single record sought by collectors, a band nearly forgotten, and an urban legend passed from punk to punk. What happened to The Fuckers on that tour? Why was their singer never seen again? No one has been able to say. Until now…

**"Zombies and Shit" Carlton Mellick III** - Twenty people wake to find themselves in a boarded-up building in the middle of the zombie wasteland. They soon discover they have been chosen as contestants on a popular reality show called Zombie Survival. Each contestant is given a backpack of supplies and a unique weapon. Their goal: be the first to make it through the zombie-plagued city to the pick-up zone alive. But because there's only one seat available on the helicopter, the contestants not only have to fight against the hordes of the living dead, they must also fight each other.

**"The Book of a Thousand Sins" Wrath James White** - Welcome to a world of Zombie nymphomaniacs, psychopathic deities, voodoo surgery, and murderous priests. Where mutilation sex clubs are in vogue and torture machines are sex toys. No one makes it out alive – not even God himself.

*"If Wrath James White doesn't make you cringe, you must be riding in the wrong end of a hearse."*
-Jack Ketchum

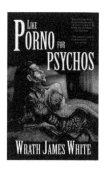

**"Like Porno for Psychos" Wrath James White** - From a world-ending orgy to home liposuction. From the hidden desires of politicians to a woman with a fetish for lions. This is a place where necrophilia, self-mutilation, and murder are all roads to love. Like Porno for Psychos collects the most extreme erotic horror from the celebrated hardcore horror master. Wrath James White is your guide through sex, death, and the darkest desires of the heart.

**"Bigfoot Crank Stomp" Erik Williams** - Bigfoot is real and he's addicted to meth! It should have been so easy. Get in, kill everyone, and take all the money and drugs. That was Russell and Mickey's plan. But the drug den they were raiding in the middle of the woods holds a dark secret chained up in the basement. A beast filled with rage and methamphetamine and tonight it will break loose. Nothing can stop Bigfoot's drug-fueled rampage and before the sun rises there is going to be a lot of dead cops and junkies.

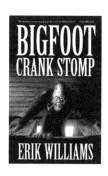

**"Survivor" J.F. Gonzalez** - Lisa was looking forward to spending time alone with her husband. Instead, it becomes a nightmare when her husband is arrested and Lisa is kidnapped. But the kidnappers aren't asking for ransom. They're going to make her a star-in a snuff film.. They plan to torture and murder her as graphically and brutally as possible, and to capture it all on film. If they have their way, Lisa's death will be truly horrifying...but even more horrifying is what Lisa will do to survive...

**"Genital Grinder" Ryan Harding** - *"Think you're hardcore? Think again. If you've handled everything Edward Lee, Wrath James White, and Bryan Smith have thrown at you, then put on your rubber parka, spread some plastic across the floor, and get ready for Ryan Harding, the unsung master of hardcore horror. Abandon all hope, ye who enter here. Harding's work is like an acid bath, and pain has never been so sweet."*
- Brian Keene

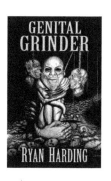

## AVAILABLE FROM AMAZON.COM

CPSIA information can be obtained
at www.ICGtesting.com
Printed in the USA
BVHW01s1442060318
509326BV00001B/49/P